Waves broke over Khan's legs, the spray flying up glittery-green and hitting my face and arms. Cold. Breakers crashed around us, striking the sand with dull booms, but Khan kept moving out. The water dragged her to a trot, then a walk, as water frothed up to her chest.

"Turn back, Khan," I said. "Enough is enough." I tried to pull her head around, but she tensed her head and neck. Might as well try to pull a steam engine around with two bits of rope.

"I think it's time to abandon ship," said Peter.

Water slopped to my knees and soaked my jeans. It was cold, like stepping into a giant freezer.

Suddenly Khan began moving in lurching motions. She was swimming!

For adventure, excitement, and even romance . . .
Read these Quick Fox books:

Springtime of Khan
Summer by the Sea

Sports Books for Girls by Dan Jorgensen
Andrea's Best Shot
Dawn's Diamond Defense

Crystal Books by Stephen and Janet Bly
1 Crystal's Perilous Ride
2 Crystal's Solid Gold Discovery
3 Crystal's Rodeo Debut
4 Crystal's Mill Town Mystery
5 Crystal's Blizzard Trek
6 Crystal's Grand Entry

Marcia Books by Norma Jean Lutz
1 Good-bye, Beedee
2 Once Over Lightly
3 Oklahoma Summer

SUMMER BY THE SEA

Marian Flandrick Bray

Chariot Books
David C. Cook Publishing Co.

A Quick Fox Book

Published by Chariot Books,
an imprint of David C. Cook Publishing Co.

David C. Cook Publishing Co., Elgin, Illinois
David C. Cook Publishing Co., Weston, Ontario

SUMMER BY THE SEA
© 1988 by Marian Flandrick Bray

Cover design by Jill Novak
Cover illustration by Joe Yakovetic

First printing, 1988
Printed in the United States of America
92 91 90 89   2 3 4 5

Library of Congress Cataloging-in-Publication Data

Bray, Marian Flandrick, 1957-
    Summer by the sea / by Marian Flandrick Bray.
       p.   cm.—(A Quick fox book)
    Summary: Sent by her father to spend the summer on
the California coast with her mother and stepfather, a
reluctant Emily, with her horse Khan, meets an unusual
young man, rescues a creature from the sea, and affirms
her Christian beliefs.
    [1. Christian life—Fiction. 2. Horses—Fiction. 3.
Divorce—Fiction.] I. Title.
PZ7.B7388Su 1988   [Fic]—dc19   88-20429
ISBN 1-555-13408-4

*to those who have loved an animal
and lost him*

Thanks to Knotts Berry Farm and Marineland, especially to Joel Silverman and his two dolphins and to Marineland's trainers Jo, Bud, and Gail. Kisses and many fish to Bubbles, the pilot whale, and to Crunch and Sundance, the Atlantic bottle-nose dolphins.

Much love and appreciation to my critique group: Maureen, who puts up with my ill temper and muttered threats, Marlys, who is logical where I'm not, and Val, who gives me chocolate and Earl Grey tea (with milk).

Also to Carol, who loves the magic in the world and is quite magical herself.

Show me your horse and I will tell you what you are.
Old English Proverb

Contents

1
The Brown Dwarf

Even as I slept, I knew it was a dream, but still it snarled around me like seaweed, pulling me in deeper. The dream was always the same.

An unborn star, veering wildly through the frozen vacuum of space, I heaved. My skin of burning hydrogen and helium barely sloughed off the darkness, trying to contract as a baby star ought. The tremendous pressure should have fired up the fission, but it didn't.

I was dying. Before I was even born.

The observer part of me demanded, *Why am I having this dream?* I wanted it to stop, because I knew how it would twist into a nightmare.

Kicking, I tried to resurface through the layers of my subconscious, but bits of glittery stars plunged me back into space, back into my infant star-body, which still tried to collapse, a star's way of gasping for breath, but it didn't work. It never did.

I knew what I was. A brown dwarf. A useless star. One that died before it ever lived. This dream was unfair!

I'm not a brown dwarf. I'm not! I'm not! I'm—

My star-body sputtered, a cascade of fire falling.

Gold, green, red, silver. An iridescent shower of my life sparking through space. Then the face floated towards me. I'd met him in other nightmares. The grinning face of death. His presence blinked out the living stars as I tried to swim free of my dying body. But his teeth caught my soul. This was it. The final dream. A scream rose in me, but stars can't scream.

Suddenly I was awake. The scream ground to a halt in my throat, as my thoughts scrambled frantically for the verse I'd memorized a few weeks ago. What was it? I couldn't remember how it started. My body was hot with sweat, and the sheets were tangled around my legs. I kicked free and lay panting, as the verse flooded into my memory: "Awake, sleeper, and arise from the dead, and Christ will shine on you."

I'd picked that one because it was pretty and because I didn't want to do the same old traditional ones. Now it lit my mind. My heart rate leveled off as I repeated the verse over and over, the words like chimes.

The fear ebbed. And awake, I realized who the brown dwarf was. Not me.

My mother.

2
Recycled Stars

I eased out of the house that morning, leaving a note on the kitchen counter for Mom and Jack, my stepfather. The blue Post-it note stood out on the white tile: *Went to see Khan. Emily.*

Outside, the marine fog clung between the canyon walls—See Canyon. What a funny name. A joke: Come to See Canyon. See the canyon? No, See Canyon.

See' Canyon was a bridge between San Luis Obispo and Avila Beach. We were closer to the beach—at least, that's what Mom said. I hadn't seen the whole canyon yet.

I hiked along the brushy path, away from the house. Despite my fancy talk before school ended last week for the summer, here I was. Two hundred and fifty miles from home, at Mom's. Exactly where I'd said I'd never go.

Even Dad, who's as stubborn as a balky horse, had given up on me.

"Fine, Emily," he said to me about a month ago. I was sitting bareback on Khan, my legs against her shoulders, my shoes brushing the upper part of her legs. "Just ignore your mother's wishes, and don't visit her."

He made me sound mean, but how could I visit her for a whole summer? I hadn't even gone to her wedding.

Khan shifted uneasily under me at Dad's angry voice and at my own frustration.

"I'm tired of arguing with you," Dad said and stalked off to mess with the plumbing in the boarder barn. I got the message. He would let me stay home, but he wouldn't let me forget it was against his will. What fun.

"Okay!" I shouted, wheeling Khan around, something I knew better than to do. She tossed her head, snorting. "I'll stay at Mom's all summer and be perfectly miserable!"

Then I dug my heels into Khan's ribs, and she leaped straight up. We parted instantly. All I could think of was: *Life is not fair.*

The ground caught me, and I rolled up off my shoulder and stood in time to see Khan run off, bucking and twisting, the reins flapping and her body a silver thread spinning away. I had the distinct feeling that this was one of God's little ironic jokes. *See, Emily, you can't even control your horse. What makes you think you can control your life?*

Give me a break, God.

But He hadn't, so here I was at Mom's.

The morning breeze feathered over me. At least I had Khan with me. That had been my last demand. I suppose Mom was humoring me when she agreed to that, but did I care? It had worked. I paused a moment, trying to remember which path led to the pasture. We had run over it last night quick. The doubled-over oak tree was familiar, so I jogged past it.

I burst through the black oaks and carefully slipped between the wire strands of the fence into the pasture.

We'd driven in late yesterday, with Khan in the double horse trailer. Ian, my older brother, drove the four and half hours from southern California. I hadn't wanted him to leave, which was a switch. Usually I considered him a pain in the behind.

"Have a good summer, Em," he said and touched my arm.

"It won't be easy."

"Be strong," he said and the rest of the verse—"in the Lord"—played out in my mind.

I gripped his forearms, and he smiled. "I don't envy you," he said. "It's tough."

He climbed into the truck and drove off. I fought tears as the trailer's red lights vanished into the night.

This morning it was the sky that fought tears.

I snapped my Levi jacket. The eucalyptus trees were shrouded in fog. Beyond the trees, the steep canyon wall jutted up. It didn't seem as though the Pacific Ocean was really only a couple miles away. It wasn't oceany enough or something.

Now where was that mare? A narrow path was worn by hooves, so I figured Khan and the other horses would be along it. The pasture was an odd shape, long and narrow, and across the back the ground crumpled up to the canyon wall.

Khan was the color of fog—the color of the ocean last night as we rounded the bend on Highway 101 just past Pismo Beach. Moonlight had silvered the fog and lit the ocean with a cast-iron look, then a shimmery jeweled look.

The fog broke a bit. I could see to the end of the pasture, which was dirt and thin grass. Khan was greedy; she wouldn't eat poor grass.

15

Turning back, I headed for the gate. A movement near the neighbor's house made me lift my head. Mom said their last name was Kjaard: a strange twist-of-the-tongue word. Out of the fog I saw the bodies of horses. A chestnut one. A spotted one. And a tall, gray one. Of course. Khan, being Khan, had figured out that the neighbors fed the horses twice daily. There she was, getting her fair share.

The mare had her dark muzzle down, nosing through the flakes of alfalfa hay, alongside the other two.

"Hey, girl," I called. She flicked her ears in my direction, but continued munching. The other two horses watched me casually, also eating. One was a chestnut quarter horse gelding with straight up and down legs, practically no fetlocks, and a big Roman nose with a droopy lower lip. The other was an Appaloosa pony, probably thirteen hands—Pony of America?—with fist-sized spots. A leopard Appy. He was very clean and tight, as if someone rode him a lot. Good. Maybe I could ride with that person.

With my fingers I combed Khan's untidy mane. "How's your little baby today?" I asked. She'd been bred last month to El Noor, who was a Polish Arabian like her. I didn't know for sure if she was in foal, but I didn't think she'd gone back into heat, so I liked to imagine a tiny baby horse floating inside her. I patted her flank gently.

The fog stirred, and the horses put up their heads. Someone sat on the gatepost, shadowy. Maybe it was an angel. It sort of looked how I imagined the angel must have appeared to Mary, when she was hunting around the graveyard for Jesus. An echoing crunch came from the figure. Right—an angel eating an apple.

"Who are you?" I called.

Another chomp. Probably one of the Kjaard kids. Mom had said there was a whole pack of them.

A boy's words came back, "I might ask you the same, since this is my pasture."

Oops.

"I'm just checking on my horse," I said.

More crunching, then the spotted pony walked up to the guy and held up his slim head. The boy dropped the apple core into the pony's open jaws and wiped his fingers on his shorts.

"Mrs. Davidman's daughter, huh?"

Mrs. Davidman was my mother's new married name. Well, not so new. Two years now. I just hadn't gotten used to it.

"I'm Emily Sowers." *Notice the different last names,* I wanted to add.

"Peter Kjaard." He dropped off the gatepost, landing lightly. He was a head taller than me, and graceful. I could see it even in simple moves. Too slim for football. Track? But he didn't have the gaunt look. Gymnastics, maybe. He rested his arms on the pony's straight back, and it kept eating as if it were used to kids hanging all over it.

"I thought you were an angel," I said and then could have kicked myself. What a stupid thing to say.

But he didn't laugh. He stared at me. His eyes were green, but not like a cat's. More like a sage's. Amused. Clever. Maybe a little wise.

"An angel might not be so bad," he said thoughtfully. "I'd like to fly around the stars."

"Both my brothers would love to be angels so they could do that," I said. "But they don't act like angels." Farley came closer than Ian.

"How about you? Wouldn't you like to fly around the stars?"

"I'm not so sure. I like the earth an awful lot."

A slow smile began over his face, beginning with his lips and trickling up to his eyes.

I thought of my dream of the brown dwarf. "I'd like to *be* a star"—but without the terror, please!—"and just be out in space."

"That's different," he said. "Most people would say they'd like to be an astronaut—or not be one. Not too many people would want to be a star."

I wasn't sure if he liked what I said or thought I was strange. I stroked Khan's neck as she ate.

"Actually," I said, knowing I was putting myself in deeper, "people are really recycled stars, did you know that?"

In a swift motion, he swung up on the Appy and leaned back as if the pony were a couch. "No, I didn't know that. How do you figure?"

"Everyone has some of the same elements in their bodies as stars. Since the stars were formed first, then us, it makes sense."

"Is your horse a recyled star?"

"Of course." In a silly, probably childish way, I was pleased he was playing along. "I think Khan is probably more like a pulsar than a regular star. Something out of the ordinary."

"Are you an out-of-the-ordinary star?"

I wished I were. "No, just a star like our sun."

"Our sun is pretty special," he said and sat back up. The pony shook his neck. The hay was nearly gone.

"Well, yeah, but it's like a lot of other stars."

"Being ordinary isn't so bad," he said. "It makes life easier."

Well, that was a bit of a sermon if I'd ever heard one. I was about to ask him what kind of star he was when a tiny voice, low to the ground, said, "Pee Pee!"

Huh? That's what Farley used to say after it was too late to use the toilet, I raised an eyebrow.

Peter slid off the pony and said over the gate, "Come here, Dawn."

A baby toddled through the grass with a wet-with-dew Border collie at her side. She held the dog's long neck fur in her fist. He seemed to be leading her. Was she blind? Her eyes looked funny. Not blank like a blind person's, but sort of unfocused. She had the same curly blonde hair as Peter.

When they reached the barbed wire, Peter pried the child from the dog and lifted her over the gate. The collie, freed from his baby-sitting, bolted, zigzagging through the rye grass.

"See the new horse, Dawn?" He pointed his fingers at Khan. She followed his fingers deliberately with her gaze. So she wasn't blind. And she was bigger than I'd first thought. More like three.

"Can she touch your mare?"

"Sure." Khan ignored us all and kept eating.

"A gray horse," Peter said to Dawn. "Pretty horse, with a long mane."

"Mmm," said Dawn, one arm around Peter's neck and her legs wrapped around his waist.

I didn't know that much about little kids, but it seemed when Farley was her size, he was jabbering in sentences. Maybe this little girl was big for her age.

"My horse's name is Khan," I said.

Dawn started, as if she hadn't seen me until now. She had strange eyes. Uncanny, as if she saw right through me.

Peter swung Dawn back and forth, and she squealed. "Let's see, Dawn wouldn't be a star, no. What would she be?" He seemed to be talking more to her than me, but I listened curiously.

"Dawn would be a quark, not a star. One of those subatomic parts. Invisible, but totally necessary." He swung her some more, making her giggle.

Totally necessary. I doubt my brothers would say that about me!

Dawn suddenly chirruped, "Hos, hos." Then, "Pee Pee."

Peter winced. "That's how she says my name. Dawn, this is Emily."

I grinned and held out my hand. "Hi, Dawn."

She stared at me, drooling. Peter put her hand in mine, and I shook her sticky fingers gently. She looked at her own hand that I was shaking slowly. Then she lifted her chin and fixed her smoky blue eyes on me and said, "Eee."

"That's close," I said, not feeling as foolish as I thought I might. "This is my horse. She's my friend."

Well, most of the time Khan and I were friends. She still reverted to her quirky nature.

Peter sniffed at the air. "Hey, is it time to change your diapers?"

Dawn shook her curly head, and Peter shifted her to his other hip.

"Oh, yes, it is." Then he said to me, "What are you doing this afternoon?"

"Getting unpacked and probably riding Khan some. My mom and stepfather work all day."

"If you want, I can show you around. Like the beach or back in the hills."

I was sure I could find my own way, but it would be fun to have Peter show me the best places. And anyhow, a guy who would change his little sister's diapers was certainly worth getting to know. "I'd like you to show me around."

He smiled. "Okay. See you about one?"

I nodded, and he slipped through the fence, Dawn still on his hip. He whistled up the dog. "Yo, Blues!"

The collie bounded past me as I headed back to Mom's. Maybe the summer wouldn't be so bad after all.

3
Saltwater Bath

Down the path, rocks sliding under my shoes, I ran for home, pushing through a scratchy patchwork of blackberries. As I scrambled up the steep dirt hill to the gravel drive, Biscuit, Mom's honey-colored cocker spaniel, yapped.

My stepfather, Jack, turned from watering his pinks and "naked lady" flowers. "Good morning, Emily," he said formally.

Biscuit kept barking at me.

"Hi, Jack," I said and crouched down. "Come here, Biscuit." The dog barked shriller.

"Go on, you dumb dog," said Jack and good-naturedly shoved his shoe into the dog's nearly tailless rump. Biscuit yelped and ran wriggling into my arms and licked my face. He was softer than Khan when she was clean and I'd put creme rinse on her fur.

Jack turned off the water and coiled the green hose. "We ought to be home around five, but if we're later, I'll have Beth call you. Make yourself at home."

Beth was my mother. "Okay." I stood, brushing the golden hairs off my legs. Biscuit wiggled at my feet, his tongue a raspberry streak. "I'm gonna find Mom."

"She's in the kitchen." He parted the flowers, hunting for weeds, I guess.

I hurried into the house. Jack wasn't a bad guy or anything. But my mom chose him over my dad, and I was supposed to be happy about that?

Biscuit ran after me. The scent of bacon sizzled in the air.

"Where have you been?" asked Mom, lifting the dripping bacon out of the pan with a fork and dropping it onto a paper towel to drain.

"I left a note," I said defensively. I always left notes for Dad. "I met your neighbor. Peter Kjaard. Do you know him?"

"I don't see the family much." She had an apron over her dress which was a lot nicer than anything she'd worn at home. It was red and silky looking, and she wore a single strand of pearls. Of course, now she sold real estate. At home she used to muck stalls and ride colts. She never wore an apron.

Home reminded me of what Dad had said: Help however you can. So I said, "I can fix breakfast every morning."

"That's an idea. Tonight when I get home we can plan a menu. How's that?"

"Sure. I'm a pretty good cook. I get lots of practice at home."

"I thought your father was going to get a housekeeper." Her voice hardened.

"The pipes in the boarder barn burst in May, so we all take turns cooking and cleaning. It's not so bad." Besides, I didn't like the idea of some stranger in our house. Dad's girlfriend, Megan, was all I could handle.

Mom cracked eggs into the frying pan. "Still like your eggs over easy?"

She remembered.

22

"Yeah." As she cooked, I flipped through *The Daily Coastal Times*. On a couple of pages a reporter's name popped up: Gregory Kjaard. Were there other Kjaard families, or was this Peter's dad?

"Does Mr. Kjaard work on the newspaper?"

"Oh, I don't know, honey."

"What are the Kjaards like?"

She set down a breakfast of neatly flipped eggs and bacon. "Nice enough. There are worse people in the canyon."

"What do you mean?" Peter did seem too good to be true.

She set down two more plates and whisked off her apron as Jack came in. "You know—people into alternative life-styles. Natural foods or odd religions." She gave a shrug.

Jack sat down beside me, picked up his fork, and said, "Greenpeace is popular among the young people. And the Abalone Alliance."

"Not just the young," said Mom and sipped coffee. They began eating without a prayer, so I said a quick one in my head. Neither of them glanced at me. Earlier I'd thought of offering to say grace, but they might think I was into an alternative life-style or something.

"Well, Peter is going to show me around today," I said. "Is that okay?"

She shrugged again. "He seems harmless. Have you seen the youngest?"

"Dawn?"

"Is that his name?"

"*Her* name."

"Okay, but she's a Mongoloid. That says something, doesn't it?"

I wasn't sure what that said. That they adopted a baby from another country? No, wasn't that a disease?

"So, Emily, what is this Peter going to show you?" Jack was trying to be friendly, but really, how was I supposed to know what Peter would show me? Just around. I didn't know. I'd never been here before. All of a sudden, as he looked at me, his face seemed strained, and I wondered if he were less than thrilled at having me here this summer.

That made two of us.

"We'll just ride around. Peter's going to show me the beach or maybe the canyon." I nibbled on the bacon. At home I made it better.

"If you go to the beach, I want you to be careful," said Mom. "It's not like swimming in a pool."

No kidding, I thought, and then I felt guilty. After all, she is my mom and she's concerned, right? If I ever have kids, I hope I have all boys. I think I'd make a lousy mother to a girl. Maybe I'd better just stick to horses.

"Peter's a good boy," said Jack unexpectedly. He wiped his mouth with the paper napkin.

We ate in silence for a few moments. Then Mom said, "I didn't have a chance to tell Emily, but I need someone to help in the office. Some canvassing, too. I thought Emily could help."

"Canvassing?" I asked, suspiciously, but the unknown couldn't be worse than working in an office.

"Leaving flyers from our office at homes, so people will know about us."

That didn't sound so bad. Maybe I could ride Khan, the way some kids deliver newspapers on horseback. But the office work sounded boring.

"You can tell Emily about it later, Babe. We'd better get going," said Jack.

Babe? Give me a break.

"See you tonight, Em," said Mom, and she gave me a fake kiss on my forehead, a loud smack. She hadn't

24

finished her breakfast. Was that why she was so skinny? She handed me their business card. "You can call us here."

It was gray, embossed with *Sea Breeze Real Estate* and my mom's and Jack's names in a fine blue script with a San Luis Obispo address and phone number.

The car engine revved up as I finished eating. Biscuit crept over, begging, his large, liquid eyes wanting food. Knowing I shouldn't, I lowered Mom's plate, and he expertly licked it clean.

The car roared away. I fought a tremendous urge to run upstairs and look through Mom's dresser drawers, her closet, trying to find something familiar about her.

What had happened to my mother?

I rinsed the plates and loaded them into the dishwasher. Modern technology. I could get used to it fast. We didn't have a dishwasher at home. Correction: *I* was the dishwasher.

After cleaning up, I looked through the newspaper's classified ads. Lots of horses for sale. Many of them cheaper than at home. Biscuit whined and sat on my feet, so while I looked, I scratched his heavy ear. Lots of Arabians for sale. I was surprised, because I would have thought in this cattle country the quarter horse would be king.

A display ad showed a lean horse and rider trotting up a hill. The ad read:

ANNOUNCING

The Black Swan Race
Win Cash Prizes

Sat. Aug. 17
Race 9 miles through the hills
and finish on the beach.

Held in honor of the famous
Thoroughbred mare, Black Swan,
who in 1852 beat Governor Pio
Pico's Spanish stallion, Sarco.

First prize—$500
Second prize—$300
Third prize—$100

All finishers will receive
a new leather halter from
Evan's Custom Saddlery Shop.
Pick up entry blanks there.

"How about that, Biscuit? I bet Khan could win it."

Biscuit licked my hand as my thoughts soared into the race. Khan running as she was bred to do, nose outstretched, mane flying. Under me she'd surge, straining to win. Exploding over the finish line.

First, of course. Second was certainly no disgrace, but I bet she could win first place. She was an Arabian, and they were bred for endurance. If Khan won this race, it would show all the people who didn't think much of her (like the people I bought her from; the people at the racetrack who banned her; her first owners, who sold her because she didn't win any of her four races; even my dad, who thought Khan was a dingy horse; and my mom, who thought all horses were dippy), that she was good and beautiful.

Five hundred dollars wouldn't be bad, either.

Biscuit settled his head into my lap. There were some problems, such as Khan possibly being pregnant. Could she still race if she were? I wasn't sure. Also her leg. She'd injured it last spring, and I didn't want her to rehurt herself. And would Mom even let me race? There was no telling.

I went upstairs and unpacked. Biscuit sniffed all my stuff, especially the bottoms of my shoes. "Silly," I told him. After I put everything into drawers, I changed into shorts and a T-shirt. Thinking about Peter, I braided my hair in the herringbone braid the way my best friend, Melissa, had taught me. I thought about curling my bangs, but I figured the wind would snatch any curls out. It wasn't worth it, even for Peter Kjaard.

Sitting on the low dresser, I stared at myself in the oval mirror. Did Peter think I was pretty? Probably not. I was still an ordinary, run-of-the-mill, G-type star. I smiled, thinking of Peter. He looked like a blue star—one of those big, hot, young stars.

I looked closer at my face. At least my skin was okay. Maybe if I wore more makeup, I'd be exotic and people would say, "Who's that beautiful girl?"

I laughed at myself. The only time I heard anything close to that was when I rode Khan and people said, "Isn't that a beautiful horse?" Oh, well. Dad was fond of saying that Khan was my alter ego. At least my alter ego was outstanding.

The clock over my bed read almost twelve-thirty, so I brushed my teeth and put the house key in my pocket. Biscuit trailed me.

"Poor dog. You get left alone all day, don't you? Want to come?"

Those were the magic words. He yelped and flung himself against me, long ears flapping. A couple of leashes were hanging on the coatrack, so I snapped one to his collar, and we ran out into the day.

At the barbed wire, I held the bottom strand up and Biscuit squirmed under, catching his ear on a prong. He yelped, but kept crawling. He probably didn't get out much. You don't get a luxuriant coat from tromping in the hills.

Carefully I slipped after him and told him, "You're in for a surprise." Maybe he'd never seen a horse before, let alone three horses.

The horses had drifted back from the gate, the hay gone. Peter wasn't around, so I tied Biscuit to a fence post and went to get Khan's grooming tools and hackamore in the stand-up toolbox under a cluster of oak trees. Biscuit began barking shrilly.

"I'll be there in a minute," I hollered, loading the tools into a rubber bucket. Biscuit kept barking. I can't stand a yapping dog. I whirled around, ready to smack him, when my mouth dropped in surprise.

Khan was standing over him, ears up, nostrils flared. Biscuit was pressed against the fence post, cowering, but barking. The mare stepped closer, head lowered. She wasn't looking at the frantic dog, but at the slip knot in the leash.

All at once I knew what she was about to do. "No, Khan! No!"

Quickly, with her long teeth, she pulled the knot free and wheeled away, the leather leash in her teeth.

"Khan, whoa!" I commanded. She just tossed her head and strode away. Great trainer, right? Biscuit followed the demanding leash, but gave me a reproachful look, tucking her stubby tail.

I started after them until, shaking with laughter, I had to hang onto the gatepost.

"What a clever horse," said a voice.

I straightened, and Peter grinned at me, one hand on his dog, the other hand holding a bucket of grain.

"Too clever," I said and dashed away to rescue Biscuit. Khan was trotting now, with Biscuit in tow.

"I'll kill you, Khan!"

She broke into a gallop, Biscuit flying after her. He stumbled, and thankfully Khan dropped the leash but fled on, bucking and flinging herself around the

28

pasture. The other two horses galloped after her.

Biscuit raced back to me. "Look at you," I said. He was covered with cockleburs. "But it doesn't matter. You're safe now." I unsnapped the leash, wiping my hand on my jeans. It was slobbery where Khan had had it in her mouth.

Peter was laughing when we came back. His dog, Blues, jumped up and sniffed at Biscuit, who'd had enough of new creatures. He backed between my legs, growling.

My gaze met Peter's, and we burst into fresh laughter. Khan *was* funny. Even Biscuit got into the mood and licked Blues's face.

"I read somewhere," said Peter, "that 'he deserves Paradise who makes his companion laugh!' Your horse is in for sure."

"I figure she'll be in heaven, because God likes horses," I said and picked some burrs from Biscuit's coat.

Peter raised his eyebrows. "Does He?"

"Sure. There's lots in the Bible about horses. Jesus rides on a white horse."

He smiled. "That's right, He does."

I smiled back. "Are you a Christian?" I asked. Melissa says when you first get saved you go crazy and talk more easily to people about that. She says I'm still sort of crazy, but I don't feel crazy.

"Yeah, I am, actually," he said.

A warm feeling rose in me. "So am I."

"Well," he said briskly, straightening. Blues heeled, his nose against Peter's bare knee. "Would you like to see the hills or the ocean?"

"Is there a charge for this tour?"

"Usually, but for you, no."

What a line! "Why no charge for me?"

He grinned. "I'm just a friendly, generous guy."

"Right." I nodded my head.

"You'll see. Now which is it? Hills or ocean?"

Hills were old friends. At home our house was surrounded by hills. "The ocean."

"Okay. Were you going to ride?"

"Is that all right?"

"Is Khan in good shape? It's about two miles to the beach."

"No problem." Last spring Khan had been frightened and leaped a six-foot fence, practically from standing still. Then she took off running. Dad estimated she must have run about twenty miles, maybe more. Aside from that, I ride her a lot.

He ducked under the fence, calling, "Here, Seal! Here, Mannie! Here, Khan!" and headed for the horses, shaking the grain which I imagined made pretty music to their ears.

Seal and Mannie came up to Peter; Khan was hanging back. Peter let the pony and the gelding take a mouthful; then, as they chewed, he called Blues over to hold back the two horses. Each time they tried to go to Peter, Blues barked and dashed at them. Mannie turned away and began grazing, but Seal stood his ground, ears flat.

Peter held the bucket out to Khan, his voice whispering words that didn't sound English. French or something. She came forward, ears up like curved half moons, eyes wide, ignoring Blues's yapping and concentrating on the grain. Slowly she pushed her muzzle into the bucket and drew back chewing. I never grained her—she already had so much energy—so this was a real treat.

With hackamore in hand, I went quietly to her. As she pulled her nose out of the bucket, chewing more grain, I put my hand on her neck. The delicate balance happened. Although she could have bolted, she didn't. She was at the point where she allowed me to bend my will over hers. I slipped the hackamore over her face and tied the throatlatch in place.

Peter retreated to the top of the gate while I brushed Khan. Dust and dandruff flew. Through Khan's pale, fluttering mane, I watched Peter staring off into space. What was he dreaming about?

He caught me looking at him and smiled.

I busied myself with Khan, fighting the heat of my face. "Hey," I said to distract him. "Aren't you going to get a horse ready?"

"Nah, I have this." He pointed to a skateboard in the grass. "It's downhill. On the way back, I'll hitch a ride."

"You better ask Khan. Last time I rode double, she sent us flying." Farley and I had tried once. We ended up in the grass, Farley draped over me and Khan with her heels in the sky.

"Is Khan her whole name?"

I whisked the dandy brush over her rounded rump. "Khan Pippa. She's a purebred Polish Arabian."

Peter gave a low whistle. "Not bad. Lots of Arabs in this area," he said. "Used to be lots of quarter horses, like old Mannie there." At his name the gelding lifted his head, asking, *More grain?* "My older sister was really into being a cowgirl, and nothing but a quarter horse would do."

"How many sisters do you have?"

"Three." He wrinkled his nose. "I can't get away from them. Hair and clothes everywhere."

"Don't like girls, huh?"

"Sisters aren't girls."

"I'm a sister. Twice over in fact."

He winked. "But not my sister."

"Good thing for you. I'd have knocked your head in a long time ago."

He chuckled.

I tossed the grooming tools into the bucket and put it outside the fence, then led Khan out. Seal and Mannie ran up behind, whinnying longingly.

"Sorry," I said and swung up on Khan's back. I gathered up the reins as Peter picked up his skateboard.

I'd wrapped Biscuit's leash around my waist because I couldn't keep him on the lead while I rode. "Come on, Biscuit," I called. "Walk time."

He followed, jumping and barking.

"Who says animals are dumb?" I asked. "They understand words."

"They do," said Peter. "I have lots of respect for animals. Especially ones bigger than me." He rested his hand on the point of Khan's hip.

We started up the path to Peter's house and to the road, when a blonde girl, ten or so, bounced down the path.

"Peter, Dad can't pick up Dawn's minerals, so Mom wants you to get them after your—"

He broke in. "I'll get them. Hey, Cassie, this is Emily. Her horse is in our pasture for the summer."

Her face was smooth and upturned, her blue eyes shiny. "I saw you unload her last night. She's really beautiful. Seal is mine. Maybe we can ride together sometime."

"Why is your pony named Seal?" I asked.

"Because he's spotted like a leopard seal. I hoped he'd like the ocean, but he doesn't. He hates water."

"I've read about Shetland ponies who actually eat seaweed and fish when they can't find food on the island," I said.

She laughed, her voice light and gold. "That's gruesome. I'm glad Seal doesn't do that. He'd have awful breath!"

32

"Let's go," Peter said to me.

Cassie called after us, "Don't forget after your—"

He interrupted her again. "I remember, pip-squeak."

"Don't call me that, bonehead."

Peter just grinned, and we went on. They reminded me of Ian, my older brother, and myself, always bickering. Dad threatened to cut out our tongues, but if he did, I bet we'd learn sign language insults.

The top of the Kjaards' driveway merged with the See Canyon road and meandered down out of the narrow canyon.

"This road runs to the ocean," said Peter. He retied his high tops, then pushed off on his skateboard. The wheels rattled over the bumpy blacktop and Khan started, snorting at the strange moving board.

"Is she afraid of cars, too?" asked Peter.

"No, she's cool." After a minute of talking to her and stroking her neck, she calmed down. Walking along the dirt shoulder, she ignored Peter and his wheels, even when they came close to us as a car whizzed past.

"Why don't you use a saddle?" he asked.

"She hates them. She used to be a racehorse, and I think the saddle reminds her of the track. Besides, the people I bought her from scared her a lot when she was under saddle. Lots of bad memories, I guess. She acts the same way with a bit in her mouth. But she's getting better." I stroked her unruly mane.

"I didn't know Arabians were raced. Did she win?"

I shook my head. "Four starts. No wins. She was banned because of rearing in the starting gates."

"I have a friend like that."

I tried not to smile, because he was so serious. "Your friend never wins?"

"Something like that." A frown crossed his face. "I've known him since sixth grade. He's always been

33

a real troublemaker. I think part of it is because he's had some tough stuff happen, and now he just reacts."

"Khan's fine as long as I remember that certain things scare her. And she used to have reason to be scared. Now I try to let her know I won't hurt her."

"Does she seem to know that you're her friend?"

I was glad he thought people and animals could be friends. "I think she does, most of the time."

The skateboard rattled down the hill. Through strands of fog, green and blue glinted.

"The ocean!" I said, sounding like a little kid. But I didn't care. The wind blew the scent of water, briny and heavy, across the road. Khan craned her head, and I drew a deep breath.

Khan snorted, one loud explosion. Her head flew up and her mane fell back like streamers of silver in my lap. I tightened my legs around her ribs.

"Stay away," I warned Peter. "She's being weird."

He rode out to the middle of the road and called the two dogs to him. Khan pranced, her hooves thudding over the dirt, then ringing over the asphalt. Usually when she got agitated, her body tightened and her ears went flat. Now she just tossed her head again and let out a long neigh. Not a challenge, but a question.

I didn't see any other horses around, but the wind must be bringing their scent. Khan walked calmer, and I lifted my hand at Peter. "She's okay now."

He sent the dogs back to the side of the road where they ran, flattened down, a streak of honey and a streak of black and white. Peter surged ahead, balancing with his elbows out, his forearms in front of him, looking a little like the sophisticated jets Ian so admired. Green pastures on both sides of the road rolled past like delicious curves of adventure. I wanted to explore it all.

"Cross here," said Peter, flipping up his skateboard

with his foot. Khan stepped daintily over the blacktop, until she reached the middle of the road. There she lifted her forefeet especially high and plopped them down with satisfying clunks.

Peter hauled Biscuit across by his collar, and Blues romped over. On the other side he let Biscuit go, and the two dogs dashed off, racing for the sand. Peter ran after them—and what else could Khan and I do?

The mare leaped along the frontage road, springing over short bushes. We fled through the sandy ground, broken by purple pigweed, and around several houses up on stilts with wooden staircases. Then, as we hit pure sand, Khan suddenly propped and half reared, her fine chisled head high. I clung to her mane, and she came down with that funny loud neigh.

"She's welcoming the ocean," said Peter.

That's what it seemed like. She wasn't angry, but dancing with pleasure.

Peter threw his skateboard into a thick green bush. "Let me on."

"She'll buck us off."

"I'll sit close, and she'll never know."

"She'll know."

"She's too excited to care. Come on."

"Don't say I didn't warn you." I backed Khan to a trash can, chained to a wooden post, and Peter scrambled up the post and onto Khan's smooth back.

I clucked, and she stepped out readily, one ear back, saying, *I know he's there, you can't fool me.* But she didn't protest.

"She's pretty upset," Peter said pleasantly in my ear.

"Shut up." I leaned closer to Khan's neck and she trotted. Maybe it would jar Peter off. His arms were around my waist—well, he had to hold on—but my heart rate had gone up about fifty million times. His arms were warm.

Khan shifted into a canter on her own, the sand spraying up sparkly under her hoofs. The dogs ran beside us, dragging their tongues.

"Easy," I said and pulled back on the reins. I was afraid she'd strain her legs or stumble in the heavy sand with the extra weight. She only tensed and headed straight for the water.

The sand flew under us. I pulled one rein, then the other, and she slowed slightly. Peter didn't loosen his hold, and my face was hot from his touch.

Khan slowed to a trot, her mane flapping in my face. The water was just a few strides away. Since most horses hated water, like Cassie's Seal, I didn't make an issue out of stopping her—I figured the waves would slow her. But Khan had to make a liar out of me again. Instead of slowing or turning, she bounced forward and hit the water in full stride.

4
The Seaworthy Man

Waves broke over Khan's legs, the spray flying up glittery-green and hitting my face and arms. It was cold. Breakers crashed around us, striking the sand with dull booms, but Khan kept moving out. The water dragged her to a trot, then a walk, as water frothed up to her chest.

"Turn back, Khan," I said. "Enough is enough." I tried to pull her head around, but she tensed her face and neck. Might as well try to pull a steam engine around with two bits of rope.

"I think it's time to abandon ship," said Peter.

Water slopped to my knees and soaked my jeans. Cold, like stepping into a giant freezer. I yelped and Peter laughed.

Suddenly Khan began moving in lurching motions. She was swimming!

A billow swept Peter off. Where his arms had been warm, cold water gurgled in. Another wave, firm as a hand slap, carried me off and I went under a moment, then came back up, gasping.

Peter shook water from his eyes. "Better than any ride at Disneyland!"

Blues paddled gamely beside us, while Biscuit yapped from shore. Khan steadily swam away from us. The mohair reins floated behind her like black and red ropes of licorice. Khan was acting totally cool, totally in control, like she'd been doing this all her life.

"Khan, you brat!" I yelled and swam after her. Blues crossed in front of me, swimming after Khan, looking like an otter. "Get her, Blues," I called.

Blues, with his strong Border collie genes, went after her with me behind.

Waves rolled around us, and Blues went under. I froze, ready to dive for him, but he resurfaced with a sneeze, salt water clinging to his long whiskers.

Peter breaststroked on the right side of Khan, and Blues and I on her left. But Khan swam on, oblivious to us all, as if she were delighting in seeing an old friend. Her little grunts and squeals of pleasure came back over the rumbling water.

I drew closer. Was she slowing down or was I really catching up to her? Her long tail floated on the surface, tangled with strands of seaweed. I grabbed for it as a wave rolled under us. Missed. I grabbed again, and my hand tightened around the coarse hair. She pulled me along without twitching an ear. I scissor kicked hard and drew even with her shoulder, so I let go of her tail and grabbed her free-flowing mane. Blues and Peter closed in steadily. I wasn't sure what poor Blues was going to do—I don't think he knew, either—because he was a heeler, and Khan's heels were about a foot under water.

Blues barked at her, and Peter swam up to her head and pulled on the wet reins. At first she tossed her head, showering Peter with water; then Peter and I pulled on the reins together and forced her to turn back.

"You silly horse," I said, clinging to her neck. "What

did you think you'd do in the middle of the sea?"

As we swam closer, Biscuit barked in high yelps, quite undignified. Blues bodysurfed in. Peter followed, neatly riding a wave onto the beach. Not so skillfully, Khan splashed ashore with me gripping her slippery back tight.

The wind was a freezing edge across my back. On shore Peter pulled off his shirt and wrung it out. I wished I could do the same. Instead I wrung my T-shirt with it still on me and squeezed the water from my hair. There wasn't much I could do about my jeans.

"What was that all about?" asked Peter, shading his eyes and looking up at me.

I twisted more water from my hair. "I don't know. I didn't even know she liked water."

"Likes it? She loves it."

Khan looked over her shoulder and whinnied at the tumbling water.

Peter put his hand on her shoulder. "A sea horse," he said.

We laughed and Khan whinnied again, long and loud, shaking her body.

Even though the sun had worked its way through the fog, the wind gave me goose bumps. Peter shivered, too.

"I have a friend who lives up on the bluff," said Peter. "We could go dry off there." Sounded good to me. "I'm going to get my skateboard," he said and ran off. When he came back, he swung up—Khan still not minding—and moved close. My heart rate kicked up.

Dumb, dumb, I told myself. *It's no big deal.* But my heart said it was.

We rode down the beach, the dogs trailing, Khan again allowing Peter to ride double. I never knew what that mare was thinking. Some horses were pretty basic; it was easy to figure out what was going on in their pea brains. But Khan—she was complicated.

She labored up the steep trail, rising through layers of colors. First gray-pearl. Then above the fog the sky brightened, dapple blue, smoky blue and higher until the sunlight shimmered white, and the sky and water were polished sapphire.

At the top of the bluff, I drew rein for Khan to catch her breath. Threads of lean fog clung to the ocean's wrinkled skin. Beyond the edge of the cliff was a two-story house, small but cozy, with large white shells in the garden and poppies growing among them. A tool-shed squatted under an oak tree, and beside it was a man hosing down a black wet suit.

"Laing!" called Peter. Blues bounded over to him, tongue hanging out, looking happy. Biscuit followed, and Laing patted both dogs. Khan stopped in front of him and snorted softly.

"Well, well," said the man. "What have we here?" He smiled, showing large, white teeth. His gray hair was wild around his head like a skewed halo, but his beard was neatly trimmed. "Four wet pups and a horse. What have you been up to, Pete my boy?"

"Hi, Laing. This is Emily and her mare, Khan, who took us swimming. Can we dry off here?"

"Of course." Laing walked closer to Khan. She jumped back from the hose. "Nice swim, lovely?" he asked her and turned the water down. Khan stretched out her neck, lips flapping, and sucked up some water. When she didn't drink again, he turned off the water.

"Emily," he said, bowing from the waist and then looking up at me. "Very nice to meet you." A gold chain slipped from under his blue work shirt collar, making him look roguish, yet I liked him right away. He looked trustworthy. No, seaworthy. That was it. He was a seaworthy person.

"The mare dump you in the drink?" Laing asked, coiling the hose. Peter dismounted, and the wind found those spots where he'd been keeping me warm.

"She just started swimming," I said.

"Perhaps there was someone she knew out there," said Laing.

I smiled at Peter, who shrugged as if to say, *Laing is sort of crazy.*

Laing held out his hand, palm up, and Khan sniffed it. He petted her firmly, as if he were used to horses.

"It's great up here," I said, "You can see out a long ways." The horizon stretched past the colors and blurred at the ends, grayish and blue, meeting the sky.

"Got yourself a trooper," Laing said to Peter. "She's admiring the view while she turns blue from the cold."

I blushed and hated myself for turning red. I wasn't Peter's!

"Come on, kids," said Laing. "Get inside and dry off."

The toolshed's Dutch door was partially open, so I peered in. It was surprisingly empty.

"I keep my wet suits in here," said Laing. Black, green, and blue wet suits hung on the walls.

"Why so many?" I asked.

He smiled. "For friends who forget theirs."

"You must have a lot of friends."

"He does," said Peter. "Everyone likes him."

"It's not quite that way," said Laing. "Put your mare here?"

"Thanks. She doesn't stand tied too well."

I led Khan inside, and she followed willingly, looking around and sniffing the wet suits. Releasing her, I went back out, shut the door, and waited to see if she'd behave. She did. After pawing the dirt floor, she got down and rolled and came back up looking pleased and quite dusty.

"Silly girl," I said. She hung her head out the Dutch door, and I felt free to leave.

Laing's house was small, but tidy, the way I'd expect a well-run ship to be. Bare beams crossed overhead. In the far corner, a ladder led up to a trapdoor. What was upstairs?

Laing came out of the bedroom. "Take off your wet clothes," he said, "and I'll toss them into the dryer."

I went into the bathroom and Peter into Laing's bedroom. The bathroom wasn't so clean. Dried sand caulked the tub. More sand gritted the floor and was piled around the baseboards.

I kicked off my clothes and wrapped the robe around me. It was way too big. I didn't take off my bra and underwear because I didn't want Peter and Laing to see them—even if Peter did have three sisters. As I tried to unsnarl my hair with my fingers—a losing battle—I examined a big shell on the windowsill. Brick red with a row of holes in a line around the crest of it. It was heavy in my hand. I turned it over, and purple and green shimmered, like mother-of-pearl. I thought it was an abalone shell, but I wasn't positive. We didn't get to the beach much at home.

I gathered up my wet clothes and took them and the shell into the living room.

Peter, in red swim trunks and a torn shirt, sat on the couch beside Laing, sipping from a mug.

"It's the sea queen," said Peter.

I stuck out my tongue at him and asked Laing, "What's this shell?"

"Good taste the girl has," he said. "It's a red abalone. Fairly rare. Abalone are good eating." He smacked his lips.

"Did you eat this one?" I felt sorry for it. What did an abalone think about?

"Nope, found that one. Hard to find one all

together." He put down his mug. "Hot chocolate?"

"Yes, please."

Laing took my wet clothes and vanished into the kitchen. I peeked out the front door and saw Khan's smooth head hanging over the toolshed door. Biscuit lay flat in the sun, and Blues was scratching his ear industriously.

"Marshmallow?" hollered Laing.

"Oh, sure," I said, stepping back from the door.

He handed me a dark blue mug with dolphins on it. I cupped the warmth and sank onto the floor, resting my elbows on the coffee table.

"So how did you two hook up?" asked Laing, settling back on the tan and green couch. He looked at me, so I answered.

"I'm visiting my mom and stepdad for the summer. They live next door to Peter. Also, I'm keeping Khan in their pasture."

"I said I'd show her around and stuff," said Peter.

"Ah," said Laing, crossing his legs at the knee. "I wish I could just meet a girl and offer to show her around."

"Why don't you?" I asked. The chocolate burned my tongue, so I blew on the drink to cool it off.

The wrinkles around Laing's eyes deepened. I'd guess him to be about forty. "Most girls would be suspicious of a man offering to show them around."

"But if that's really what you meant," I said.

Laing laughed. "Perhaps I'm not entirely as honorable as Peter here."

Peter blushed, which I thought was pretty funny.

"Someday you'll find a great wife," said Peter. "Cassie prays for you every day, and she figures if God doesn't answer soon, in a few years she'll be old enough to marry you."

Laing laughed. "I will wait for her."

He seemed the type of person who just might.

"Are you a fisherman?" I asked. I could imagine him fishing with rough, woven nets, like in the paintings of Jesus and the apostles.

"I wish my life were that simple," he said. "No, I do environmental impact reports for the Coastal Commission and other agencies."

"Isn't Diablo Canyon Nuclear Plant near here?" I asked.

"Just a couple of bays over," said Peter. "Wrong switch and ka-boom. We all wake up dead."

"Thank you, Peter," said Laing drily, "for that mini-editorial. Like father, like son."

I thought Peter would laugh, but his face grew stormy and his eyes looked like tossed green waves.

"Buck up," said Laing lightly. "Fathers don't always know best."

Peter gave me a grim smile. "My dad works for the daily paper, and he's very pro nuclear. Unfortunately, that's not the only thing we don't see eye to eye on these days."

So. It *had* been Peter's father whose name I saw in the newspaper.

"That's all right," I said. "My mom and I don't get along too well, either."

"How about you, Laing?" asked Peter. "Did you get along with your parents?"

He tipped back the rest of his chocolate. "Beautifully," he said.

It must be nice, I thought gloomily.

He shook back his wild hair and added, "I ran away from home when I was fourteen. Life was easy without them."

"Great," said Peter. "Emily and I will just run away. Believe me," he said darkly. "I have thought of it."

I had, too, but I didn't say anything.

"I'm not telling you to do that—it just happens to be what I did. Went crazy in the early sixties. What a time to live."

We finished our chocolate, and Laing got our dry clothes. I changed in the bathroom and carefully put back the red abalone. Again I tried to unravel my hair, but gave up. Nothing but a shower and creme rinse would help it.

When I came out, Laing and Peter were standing outside on the small front porch. When the screen door banged, Peter looked over at me, his face uneasy.

"Um, Emily, I have to get into San Luis Obispo. Laing's going to drive me. I didn't realize how late it was. Do you think you can get home by yourself?"

"Sure. It's not that complicated." What was he going to do? Pick up Dawn's minerals. Cassie had started to say more, but he had stopped her. It seemed rude to leave me, but I could certainly get home on my own.

Laing looked unhappy. The glitter was gone from his eyes, and he ran restless fingers through his hair. "Come back and visit, Emily. I'm glad to have met you."

"Thanks for the dry clothes and hot chocolate."

I let Khan out of the toolshed and swung up. Peter whistled to Blues and said, "Go home. Go home with Emily."

Nudging Khan with my heels, I rode across the grassy area to the trail, calling to the dogs, who ran after me. Khan grunted as she dropped down the path gnarled with roots and rocks. Why was it that it was harder going downhill than up? There must be a hidden meaning in that, somewhere.

The beach was more crowded. People were walking, throwing Frisbees, running with kites, digging holes. Sunlight ran along the strip of wet sand. The fog was gone. A sudden slash of iridescence on the sand made me pull up Khan; she halted, throwing her head.

As I slipped off, Biscuit swiped me with his tognue. I picked up the shell, heavy with sand, and knocked it free. A piece of abalone? Not a whole piece, like Laing's, but a curve of one side. It fit in my palm. The outer side was olive green like an avocado, but inside it was more beautiful than Laing's shell. A soft metallic look—blue, purple, scarlet.

I showed it to Khan. "Nice, huh?" She licked it. "Silly," I said. I shoved it into my pocket and jumped back on.

We rode on home, stopping once so I could sweep up Biscuit, who'd lain down in a mustard plant and refused to get up. I plucked him out of the plant, the sticky leaves clinging to his long fur. Clumsily I remounted and rode on, balancing the limp cocker spaniel across Khan's withers.

After settling Khan in the pasture and brushing her, I talked with Mannie and Seal and stroked their soft noses. Then I thanked Blues for his company, in the end more charming and lasting than his master's, and picked Biscuit up and carried him home.

Mom's car was in the driveway. What time was it? The sun was still several hours from setting. She sat at the kitchen table, smoking. I didn't know she smoked.

"What's wrong with Biscuit?" she asked, stubbing out the cigarette.

He did look about half dead. "Tired. We went for a long ride."

"You took him with you?"

"Yeah. Was that okay?"

"Emily, that dog is a show dog. His coat is ruined."

Show dog? I looked at him in my arms, exhausted, twigs in his fur. Oops.

"That's why I gave you my business card—so you could call and ask questions." She lit another cigarette, and I got nervous. She didn't look like my mom. Maybe she was a clone. Maybe there was a radiation leak at Diablo Canyon, and she was altered.

"I didn't know there was any question about walking him. I didn't think it would be a problem."

"Next time, think."

Gads. That was like a teacher saying, *Why didn't you look up the misspelled word?* Well, I would have, if I thought it was misspelled, but why look it up if I thought it was okay? My mouth closed around the words, "I'm sorry." I set the dog down, and he wearily put his head on Mom's knee.

"What's done is done, but I'm not happy about this." She snuffed out the barely smoked cigarette against the ceramic ashtray. She lifted up a tuft of his fur, and it stayed up as if it'd been moussed. I repressed a hysterical giggle.

"I can wash him, Mom. It's all right."

She stood, Biscuit's chin falling off her knee. "It's not all right," she snapped.

Poor Biscuit had seemed to have such a good time, too. "Where would you like me to wash him?"

"I wouldn't. I'll call the groomers."

I started to say, *I can do it, really*, but I shut my mouth and stroked Biscuit's head.

Mom punched a number into the phone and made an appointment. Biscuit wriggled across my lap, and I picked leaves and foxtails from his fur. Foxtails are dangerous, so I made sure I got all of them out. I didn't know why Mom had to call the groomers. I would have done a good job.

After she hung up, I said, "I groom about ten horses at home. I could have groomed one little dog."

"Your father takes advantage of you. I don't like it."

"Dad doesn't take advantage of me. I like helping."
And I did. At home I felt useful, a part of everything.

"Enough talk. Let's pick up Jack and drop the dog off at the groomers. Why don't you run and brush your hair? You look as bad as Biscuit."

My face heated up, and I hurried upstairs. I didn't want to be here, Peter or no Peter. I wanted to go home. This lady was someone I didn't know. And I didn't like her.

5
Appointment with the Sea

After dinner, I wiped down the counters while Mom finished rinsing the dishes. I'd offered to clean up by myself, but she said no. I wouldn't have minded except she was being too polite, as if to get back at me.

"Where's Biscuit?" asked Jack.

"Sleeping." A pile of exhausted blond fur lay under the coffee table. Between the jaunt and the groomers, he'd slept through dinner.

Mom told him what I'd done. Of all things, Jack laughed and said, "Good for you! That dog needs to live like a dog for once."

Mom frowned and closed the dishwasher. "He's an expensive animal, Jack."

"So? He's still a dog."

I glanced over at Biscuit, who'd raised his head. I swear he was smiling. Then he flopped back down.

Mom started the dishwasher and came into the living room. Jack put his feet up on a flowered blue and white footstool, and I curled up on the couch with stationery to write to Melissa. Mom sat in an easy chair and lit a cigarette.

"So what's in store for you this summer, Emily?"

Jack asked. He was a trim man. Dad was slender from hard work, but Jack was trim because it was his style.

Before I could answer, Mom said, "Emily's going to come to the office and help us."

I was?

"Good," said Jack. "We're incredibly backlogged with filing."

Filing! I'd sooner slit my wrists. Mom went on as if she was telling me something happy. "I know. She could come three or four days a week and help."

Spend my summer in an office? No way. "But, Mom," I said, trying not to sound hysterical, which I was, and trying to be reasonable because I was supposed to pull my weight around here. "Maybe I could help you two days a week or even one. I have to train Khan."

Now where did I get that from? I wasn't sure Khan could race.

"Train Khan for what?" She looked at me from behind the smoke curls with that look in her eye I remember from when we were little kids and told her lies.

"Train Khan for what?" she repeated.

The words rolled off my tongue like I'd been practicing—was it a lie? I didn't think so, because as soon as I said it I knew it was true—but I hadn't even thought of it until now. "I'm training Khan for the Black Swan race."

"The what race?" asked Mom.

"We saw that once, Beth," said Jack. "Before we were married."

"The Black Swan race," I repeated. "Khan is a racing horse, after all. Besides, it would be good experience for me." I almost said fun, but doing fun stuff doesn't always go over with parents. Stuff that provides "good experience," they love.

"Since when are you interested in racing that horse?" asked Mom, blowing out smoke.

"Since I saw the ad. But," I added hastily, "I've thought about it a lot—well, some."

She leaned against the counter. "There are other things in the world besides horses."

But horses were practically the most interesting.

"Your father is so wrapped up in his horses—"

I broke in coldly. "My father does an excellent job." And he did. He had to turn people away who wanted him to train their colts.

"Exactly," said Mom. "He does his job too well."

I hated what she was implying. That my father was totally absorbed in his work. "He spends time with us." He did. Some of the time. "We go to church together and stuff."

She crossed her arms over her chest. "That's another thing. I don't like your father becoming a Jesus freak."

"He's not a freak!"

Jack got up. "Well, I think I'll mosey on out to the yard." He disappeared.

Mom faced me. "Okay, I don't mean that he's a freak. I just don't like the idea of him tangling you kids up in some religious thing."

"He didn't. We wanted to become Christians."

"That worries me even more."

"Mom, becoming a Christian is the best thing that ever happened to me." My heart began to thud so it hurt. Was this the big moment? My chance to tell Mom the Gospel? The time when she'd change from a brown dwarf to a living star?

"I do want the best for you, Emily, believe me. But religion isn't the answer. It's a crutch."

I couldn't believe she meant that. Of all the old lines. "Mom, I have a relationship with Jesus. It's not some spacey religion."

She held up her hand. "I really don't want to hear about it, okay? I'm just trying to tell you my reservations."

I wished we had a better relationship. If we did, maybe she'd be more interested in how and why I became a Christian. Maybe I should have gone to her wedding. But I'd been so crushed.

"I've got some paperwork to do," she said. "I better get to it."

She walked by me. I caught her scent, not perfume, just her. I remembered how she'd smelled when I was a baby, and she'd hold me.

"If it means anything to you, we do pray for you. Dad especially."

She didn't answer me, just walked upstairs.

The next morning I fixed breakfast, scrambled eggs and toast. No one said much. Mom had stayed upstairs all night, and I'd gone to my room and written to Melissa about what had happened.

Jack said, too heartily, "Good scrambled eggs." Big deal. Any imbecile could scramble eggs.

As they sipped coffee, Jack flipping through the newspaper, and Mom reapplying rose-colored nail polish—I was dying to know if those were her real nails or the acrylic things—Mom said, "Tomorrow I'd like you to start working at the office." She capped the bottle.

Tomorrow! I turned off the hot water. That was so soon. "How many days a week did you want me to work?" I asked, hoping she'd change her mind.

"Three, maybe four."

I would absolutely die. No question about it. I'd be like a wild animal captured for the zoo and die in captivity. "That's a lot." I tried not to squeak out the words. "Could we make it two days a week? I wanted time to train Khan." Besides, what was the difference between her working me to death in an office and Dad making me slave away in the barns? I didn't dare ask her that, but it seemed to me it was the same thing.

"We'll see," she said, not looking me in the eye. I hated that. Parents do that to have control. "Did you bring any dresses?"

"Some for church."

"Ah, yes, church."

My stomach flipped like it does in an elevator, but she didn't say any more about religion.

"We'll go shopping tomorrow and get some dresses," she said.

"You don't have to do that," I protested, mostly because next to working in an office, I hate shopping—unless it's for bits and saddles.

"Jeans won't cut it at the office," she said. She and Jack got up to leave, and Mom added, "Don't take Biscuit out again." As if she had to tell me.

"Pity the dog," said Jack. I half smiled at him.

Mom whirled on him. "You know that dog can't go trooping all over the countryside. He's got some shows coming up."

"I know, I know." Jack held up his hands as they went out the front door. "I just feel sorry for him." He took Mom's arm and they were gone.

I finished the dishes and wiped down the counters. They had a housekeeper that came in once a week, so I didn't have to do housework like I did at Dad's. All I had to concern myself with was Khan—and not forget about God in all this craziness. Why was it so hard to do, though?

Upstairs I stuck some stuff into my backpack—a towel, a sweatshirt—and went back downstairs. I added some granola bars and dried fruit. Then I left a note: *Went to beach with Khan. Emily.*

Biscuit whined after me, and I quickly shut the door. I hated leaving him. Shouldering the backpack, I wondered if Peter would be there. If he wasn't, should I knock on the door and ask for him? Then I remembered how he just took off from Laing's and decided, *Nah.* If we were going to be friends, he didn't end it too well.

Khan nickered to me and let me slip on her hackamore without making me chase her around.

"How would you like to be an endurance horse?" She pricked her ears, all fuzzy inside. As a racehorse, I bet she'd looked trimmed up. Streamlined. Now she wasn't fat, she just wasn't as tight as she could be. "I'll even run with you," I said. "We'll get in shape together." I thought about her being in foal and decided to check with Dad, even though wild horses ran all over the place heavy with foal.

As I groomed her, I checked her carefully, running my hands over her legs, feeling for heat—signs of swelling or injury—and sniffed at her frog—a bad smell was a sign of thrush—but her feet were firm and the frog springy. With the hoof pick stowed in my backpack, I was ready and led her out of the pasture.

We strode past the quiet house and out onto the road. The fog had lifted earlier, swirling like hot water in a kettle. I'd seen it from my bedroom window.

A few cars whizzed past us. Overhead a chicken hawk lazily flapped. Right in front of us, practically under Khan's hooves, a rabbit shot by, his white tail up, ears back, running frantically across the road and into the rye grass. The chicken hawk flowed closer but didn't dive, I suppose because Khan and I were there. We saved the rabbit's life by being in the right place at the right time. I wished I could be in right places more often.

Instead of going the way Peter had taken us, I rode

Khan across the highway up to the town of Avila. The streets were quiet, and Khan's hooves clip-clopped past little motels and funny, angled apartment buildings. Then we turned onto the main road through the downtown, which was only about a block long, and rode past Sal's Seafood, where its neon sign flashed in the morning light, and some other places that looked like sleazy bars.

Some guys stood around one dive, talking and smoking and leaning up against the gray clapboard. Their surfboards were propped up next to them. They leered at me. There was nowhere for me to go except past them or back the way I came, and the stubbornness in me didn't want some creepy guys to scare me away from the beach.

"Hey, baby," called one guy.

I refused to look at them, but my face burned.

"What a pretty horse you have," said another voice.

"She's not bad herself," added another.

We were almost around them. Khan was swinging her head and staring at their brightly colored surfboards.

"Wait a minute," said one, and he broke away from the group, amidst jeers and catcalls. "I just want to talk. You're a cute girl."

"I don't want to talk," I said and guided Khan out into the middle of the street. But he stepped off the curb. His hair hung to his shoulders, pale blond and stringy. I said, "I've got an appointment to keep." An appointment with the sea. Why did there have to be creeps around nice places—"Here there be dragons," as Ian often said.

"You're cute. Don't worry. I'm a nice guy, really." Sure. He smiled. He had teeth like a wolf. No, thanks. I tightened the reins slightly, about to clap my heels into Khan, when he grabbed for her.

55

As his fingers curled for the mohair hackamore, I whirled Khan away and drummed my feet into her sides. Like a blast of hot desert wind, she leaped—just like a *ballotade*, a movement of the Lippizaner—and we were free of the guy. His laughter rolled after us, and he called, "I'll catch you yet!"

6
The Dark Wave

Fearfully I looked back, but he wasn't running after us. I guided Khan off the street and onto the sand and cantered her to the shore. Nothing like that had ever happened to me before, and I was scared. As we approached the water, a dog joined us. Blues! He craned his head and gave me a doggy smile.

Slowing Khan, I checked around, but the guys weren't in sight. Thank God. What if he had caught me—what would they have done?

"Where's Peter?" I asked Blues. He barked and pranced beside us. I shaded my eyes and saw someone down by the stream where the seawater rushed inland along a riverbed.

I decided not to tell him what had happened. I was stupid to have even gone near them. It would never happen again.

Peter waved and climbed up out of the riverbed. "Hi," he called. The wind teased his curls and made him look younger. Something about him sort of glowed, like he had a lot of energy. He reminded me of Cobol, a colt I helped Dad train. Very honest and willing to give everything for what you asked. Peter seemed that way, even though he did take off suddenly yesterday. Maybe it was an emergency or something. What did I know?

I waved back and halted Khan at the edge of the mini-bank. "Whatcha doing?" I asked.

"Just looking around. Sometimes really good shells get washed up here."

"I'd like to find an abalone shell like Laing had," I said. "I found a piece of one yesterday, but that's all."

"This beach is pretty well picked over," he said. "What are you doing here?"

"Just riding around. Well, actually, I'm getting Khan in condition for the Black Swan race." I tried to sound casual, like, *Oh, yes, I do this kind of thing often.*

"That's great." He sat on the sand, his arms around Blues. "Do you think she'll win?"

"Maybe, if she wants to. She tends to do what she wants."

He smiled, and I realized with a shock that he was really cute. Melissa would say, *Of course he is. Did you just figure it out?* Yeah. I'm rather backwards.

"How old are you?" I asked suddenly.

"Fifteen."

"So am I." I'd just turned fifteen two weeks ago, and it seemed so much older than any other age I've been. Sounds obvious, but fifteen is almost sixteen, and at sixteen the world changes. Driver's license. Halfway through the teen years. Fourteen was babyish.

"Do you want to go swimming?" he asked.

"Sure." I'd packed a towel in my knapsack and worn my bathing suit under my clothes. "But I have to figure out what to do with Khan."

"Can't you hobble her or tie her?"

"I don't know if she's ever been hobbled before." And I didn't want to experiment now. When we broke

58

the colts to hobbles, sometimes they threw themselves over backwards. Those were the colder-blooded horses. With Khan being a hot-blooded horse, a fast hobbling lesson would be a disaster.

"Could you turn her loose? There aren't too many people over here."

I twirled a strand of hair, thinking. She probably wouldn't bother any people, and it was true, most of the sunbathers and moms with kids were down by the pier. "I'm not sure."

"We could go to the bay around this bluff," said Peter. "It's sort of a natural corral. Blues could guard the one side that goes back to the beach."

Dad always said trust your horse as far as you think he's able. Maybe I could trust Khan, with Blues' help. But what if she went into the sea again? And why had she done it in the first place?

"Let's see this bay," I said finally.

Peter got up and sprang lightly through the river of sea and fresh water. I followed, Khan sloshing through the water. She didn't act like she wanted to start swimming out to sea, so maybe it had been a fluke thing yesterday.

The bay was a shallow curve, like the lip of a seashell, against the hollow of the bluff that rose nearly straight up. A slip, complete with outboard motorboat, bobbed offshore. A heavy wooden plank led to it.

"This is Laing's slip," said Peter. "But it's my boat, *The Sparkle*."

"Really? All yours?"

He nodded, looking pleased, his green eyes shining like the sea with light slanting over it. "I earned the money myself. Laing lets me keep it here because his boat's over at the marina."

"How did you earn the money?"

"Oh, doing different stuff." The light fell from his eyes, and he turned away. Blues sat next to him, one ear up, one down.

In other words, we won't talk about it anymore. Okay. I got the message. But I couldn't figure him out. If I were brave, I'd say, *Okay, Peter, what's this secret you seem to have?* But he'd say, *What are you talking about? I have no secret.* Maybe I was misreading him. I hardly knew him.

Peter pulled off his shirt and tossed it into the boat. He tossed his tennis shoes in, too. I wished there were a bush to hide behind, but I tried to be a free spirit and pulled off my clothes, moving toward Khan so she partially hid me. My bathing suit was new. Black and red. Peter was looking at me, and I turned my back on him to untie Khan's hackamore. My face was probably as red as my suit.

"Easy girl, stay right here," I said, stroking Khan's neck. She didn't bolt, but lifted her head, her mane falling back like a girl's long hair. Her ears pricked upright, and she stared out at the endless churning waves. What was out there?

Then she swung her head to some grass that was fighting its way from the foot of the bluff, and I began to relax. She'd be okay loose.

"What are those islands?" I asked.

"Just a pile of rocks," said Peter. "We could go out there sometime. You'd have a better chance of finding some abalone shells."

I was about to ask him another question when Khan walked by us, her long tail swinging over her hocks. She halted at the edge of the shore, head up, ears shot forward, and I knew I had made a big mistake.

"Khan, don't you dare. Khan!"

She stepped into the small waves, flicking her tail. In just a few strides, she was swimming.

Peter shouted for Blues to get her, and we both ran after the mare. The cold shocked my legs, but I plunged in anyhow. The water was so biting that I gasped for breath.

Khan steadily paddled. Swells rose and fell. In the trough of some breakers, I couldn't see my mare and that made me panicky. Then I'd cut through the water and there she'd be, her fine gray head bobbing and her mane a circus of silver, mixing with the sea.

Beyond the breakers, the water smoothed out. I tried not to be frantic. That would make me tired sooner. I calmed myself, quieting my body. Consciously relaxing. I offered a strand of prayer to God: *Please help, okay?* Always the firm answer: *Okay, I'm here.*

Peter did a neat Australian crawl beside me, but I sort of dog-paddled and breaststroked. I'd never been out so far in the sea. "Khan! Whoa!"

No good. Her ears flicked, but she continued paddling. What if she got tired? How could we drag her in?

The shoreline curved to the north, rocky, bulging as if concealing a great secret. Ahead was an island, and Khan seemed to be heading for it. No way could I swim that far! Blues swam in front of us, but he wasn't getting any closer to her.

I was getting tired, but I didn't want to admit it or turn back. My arms and legs grew heavy. Peter pulled ahead of me. Water kept splashing into my face, and I choked on the burning salt.

I tried keeping my head up higher, free from the water, but then I'd sag back exhausted. Khan slowed down. Peter was closer to her. She began swimming back and forth, not moving ahead. I thought I saw a dark area in the water that she didn't want to pass. My heart started to pound. Shark?

Khan nickered. Not a scared nicker, but a welcoming call like she gives when she sees Bottom, Dad's gelding. A greeting.

But who was she greeting?

I caught up to Peter, who was treading water with one hand, the other hand shading his eyes. "What is Khan doing?"

Now she was swimming around the long dark spot, but not too close to it. Weird thoughts chased through my mind. Aliens in a pod land in the sea. A shark playing possum, ready to get us. Neptune, the god of the sea, coming to talk to us. I ran my hand over my face, scooping back my wet hair. I *was* getting tired. I watched the dark spot and thought I saw a head. It and Khan were touching. . . .

"Something isn't right," said Peter.

"What do you mean?"

"I'm not sure." He broke off, glancing at me. "Tired?"

"Yes."

"Why don't you float here? Relax. I'll go get Khan."

He swam off, and I didn't tell him that I can't float. I sink. But I attempted to relax, turning onto my back, taking deep breaths, and fighting the rising panic. I tried not to look at the shoreline, far away as distant mountains. *God won't let me drown,* I told myself. *Will He?* Maybe He'll send a big fish to swallow me like He did for Jonah. *Could I amend that, God? I don't want to be swallowed. How about a big fish to give me a lift?*

Peter yelled something, and I rolled off my back. Khan was still swimming around the spot, her greeting gone. Now her anxious nickers came over the waves. Maybe if I could latch onto Khan, she could carry me back to shore. At least I could rest by holding her.

Determinedly I swam for the mare and Peter. I'd

almost reached them, and saw that the dark spot was deeper than I'd realized. I was hoping it was just a batch of seaweed, when it thrashed.

Peter yelled again, and I froze, terrified, sure it was Jaws coming to get me.

Water boiled up around the spot, the darkness shrinking, then widening, and suddenly rising out of the water like a phantom. Only this ghost had a large eye which stared right at me.

I started to scream, when the wake from the thing slapped me in the face and I choked on the water. The object suddenly vanished, and after it a tail broke the surface and it was gone.

A dolphin? No, way too big. A whale? I coughed more and wiped the water from my eyes. Ringlets of waves curved out from where the beast had been.

I looked for Peter. He had grabbed Khan's neck and clung to her. She was still nickering, her ears upright, listening. Peter tugged at her mane, directing her towards me. An arm's length away, and I grabbed for her mane, then Peter hauled me closer and we hung onto her as if she were a piling from a pier.

What relief. Nothing ever felt better than to stop swimming and let Khan carry me. Her throat quivered with more whinnies. She didn't act the least bit tired, but her nostrils flared wide and showed the red lining. Of course I couldn't tell if she was sweating, and I was panting too hard to even try to count her heartbeat.

"A whale," said Peter. "Did you see her?"

Did I see her? That whale's eye, staring into mine, will remain with me forever.

Khan whinnied as the whale surfaced again, blowing air from its blowhole. It looked odd, like stuff was on its skin. Did whales have barnacles? These looked more like lines running along its head, which was black and bulbous, nothing like a dolphin's. The lines of white ran back to its dorsal fin and blended into the white hazy patch around its fin.

The whale breeched, drawing its body halfway out of the water, and coming down with a huge splash that sent waves nearly over my head. It was about three times as long as a dolphin I'd seen at Sea World.

"Look at that," said Peter. "A gill net. She's caught in a gill net. It'll kill her if it doesn't come off."

I wasn't sure what a gill net was, but it didn't sound good. "How can she get it off?"

"She can't," said Peter. "It has to be cut off."

The whale puffed out her breath again, squealing at the same time, sounding like tiny Mickey Mouse voices. For some reason I wasn't scared. I understood animals who needed help.

"Then we've got to cut it off," I said, strength flooding back to my limbs. I could swim all day if I had to. Well, almost all day.

"Let's go back to shore," said Peter. "We can't help her if we're drowning."

Reluctantly I tugged at Khan's mane. "Back to shore, Khan," I said, and surprisingly she turned. What Peter said made sense, but I hated leaving the whale. Could whales drown? Sure. They were mammals, like people.

A long whine followed us. It sounded like a shortwave radio being turned on. Khan raised her upper lip and nickered.

I swam away from Khan for a while, but that deadness of limb returned, so I grabbed her mane and let her haul me in. Onshore, I slid off her back and felt like the Little Mermaid. Dazzled. My legs were shooting with pinpricks of pain when I walked. But I was sure what we had to do.

"Your boat," I said to Peter.

He nodded. "I've got some pliers or a knife."

He rummaged around in a rusty tackle box while I dried off with my towel. Khan rolled in the powdery sand and stood, the sand clinging to her like golden sparkles. I watched for the whale and thought I saw her breech again. "What kind of whale is she?"

"Pilot whale. Darn. My tools are mostly up at Laing's."

"We can ride Khan up and put her in the toolshed and come back down," I said.

"Sounds good."

We scrambled onto Khan, Peter's arms tight around my waist, and I put my heels into her sides. At the top of the bluff, I slowed Khan, and we searched for the whale. "I don't see her," Peter said.

"Me, either. Is she all right?"

"She was swimming pretty good. At least she was coming up to the surface to breathe. The worst thing about those nets is that they tangle the animal, so it can't even get to the surface."

"So this one isn't too tangled?"

"It was hard to tell." We cantered past Laing's house. "But they get more and more tangled as they swim and fight it."

At the toolshed, we jumped off and put Khan in. "I'll go see if Laing is here," said Peter. I settled Khan in the shed the best I could, and wiped her down with some rags in the corner.

Peter came back with pliers. "Laing's gone, and the door's locked. I didn't bring my key. Darn." He leaned on the Dutch door. "We should really call the Coast Guard or Greenpeace to come help, but I'm afraid that by the time we find a phone, the whale might be gone."

Or drowned, I added silently. "We can do it," I said.

"Yeah. I just don't want you to get hurt."

"Don't be so noble," I said. "I'm tough."

He grinned and we pulled down wet suits until we found ones that fit us.

A verse trotted around in my head, I think from Psalms or Proverbs. "A righteous man (girl, too) cares for his beast." Khan was my beast, and I cared deeply for her. But this whale—this tangled pilot whale. Was she my beast? She was a wild creature. Yet I thought of Jesus' parable about the Samaritan and the neighbor. Who is my neighbor? Not just the person actually next door, but people at school, along the road (even those yucky guys? I hoped not). So why not caring for animals other than your own?

"I hope Laing doesn't mind us using his stuff." I had a feeling he wouldn't.

"Not when he finds out what it's for."

Blues sat panting at Peter's feet. "Stay here, Blues," he commanded. "Guard Khan. We'll be back." Blues slid down in the dirt outside the toolshed in a sliver of sunlight. Khan poked her head over the door, her eyes bright.

"You crazy horse," I said. "You knew, didn't you? You knew about the whale." And yesterday. Had the whale been there then?

Back down the trail. My feet were burning up. We scrambled down and searched the sea.

Please let it be there, Lord. Then I remembered my wish when Khan and I had scared off the hawk before it got the rabbit: I want to be at the right place at the right time. And I guessed we were.

The waves swelled and splashed against the dock. Under the water a shimmer of iridescence showed, but sand mingled with it and it was gone.

Peter started *The Sparkle*, and I hopped in.

7
Whale Tow

As the motor revved, Peter untied the mooring ropes and I got settled in the front of the boat. The stern? The bow? I didn't know. The only time I'd been in a boat was at Disneyland's "Motorboat Cruise," which hardly counted.

Peter took hold of the rudder, and the boat roared out of the slip. I hoped the noise wouldn't scare the whale away. Peter tapped the plastic gauge near his elbow. "We have enough gas, unless she's dived and gone farther out."

"How do you know it's a she?" I asked.

"I don't. I guess it's a habit. You know, people say about whales, 'there she blows.' "

"How far can she swim with the net on?"

He shrugged. "I really don't know that, either. But the more she swims, the more tangled she'll get."

The wind burned through my damp hair. A jillion questions darted through my mind like a school of wriggly minnows, but I didn't want to bother Peter while he was trying to motor out past rocks and through the breakers.

The little boat bashed into the waves, and the spray

curved like Khan's tail, silver and fierce. I swayed with the rhythm, feeling comfortable, the boat surging like a horse's extended canter.

Beyond the breakers, I asked Peter, "I thought whales were protected. Why are there nets for them to get caught in?"

He gave me a grim smile, his eyes dark like the sea before a storm. "They're supposed to be protected. But it doesn't always work that way."

I wondered why it was that important rules always had "outs," ways to escape them. Like the Bible says we're supposed to love people, but inside you don't want to at all, and when you don't love someone who needs it, life goes on. The rules get broken, and no one seems to be able to stop it.

"What did you call the net? Gill net?"

"Yeah. Gill nets are for catching fish. They're really huge, some five miles or more. Fishermen string them across the sea and anchor them with weights so they hang down into the water, sometimes all the way to the floor of the ocean. Anything that swims along gets caught in it, including dolphins, sea lions, and whales."

"Can't the animals see it?" I tried to imagine swimming along, then seeing this huge webbing across the ocean. It was scary.

"No. The nets are made so they can't be seen. Otherwise the fish would swim in the other direction. They aren't stupid."

"How do you know so much about this?" I asked.

"It's another thing my dad and I don't agree on. I think gill nets should be regulated more, but he's on the side of the fishermen. He doesn't worry about the animals."

"But it's not fair to the whales and dolphins!"

"I know. But as my dad would say, people are more

68

important than some incidental catch. Unfortunately, thousands of whales are caught."

"Can't anything be done?" I looked around, as if expecting to see hundreds of fishermen with gill nets, so I could do battle with them. All I saw was empty water.

Again Peter shrugged. "If a whale gets caught, the fishermen are supposed to call the authorities and to cut them out. And a lot do. I shouldn't be so hard on everyone, but it's those few who don't. And who knows, our whale could have been caught by a gill net that was ghost fishing—just loose in the sea. It's impossible to tell."

Peter cut the engine. I gave him a questioning glance.

"She's probably afraid of the boat. And this is about where we were."

The shore was far away—people there were the size of GI Joes. I was impressed all over again at Khan's swimming. Mine, too!

Seaweed floated in clumps around us. A few gulls and a pelican flapped by. No whale in sight.

I puzzled over the gill nets. "Why can't the government monitor the use of the nets?"

"It's not just the U.S. It's other countries. Who knows? Maybe the net she's caught in is from Japan or Norway."

Gill netting sounded as tangled as the nets themselves.

A rush of thin air made us turn. "On the right side," I said softly. Her dark head had broken the surface. That eye was looking at us. "Easy, girl. It'll be okay if you stay there."

She floated quietly, her bulbous head on the skin of the water.

"They have great hearing and eyesight," he said.

Had she been watching for us? Maybe it was Khan

she wanted. Perhaps the animals knew each other. Could that be? Had Khan known her as a foal in Florida? That was pretty farfetched.

Peter lifted the anchor and dropped it over the side. It plunged into the sea with a wet thud. The whale dived beneath the surface.

"Darn," said Peter. "I didn't mean to scare her." He bit his lower lip, looking less confident than I'd seen him.

I took a deep breath, hung over the side of the boat, and stuck my head under the water. It was like heavy air, green and gray. The line of the chain ran down at an angle like a telephone wire. The salt water stung my eyes. Shafts of blurry sunlight penetrated, but didn't particularly light up the water. An alien world. I wondered if we even had business messing with it. Yet someone already had, and the whale needed to be freed from that intrusion.

Gasping, I pulled up, water streaming down my hair and body. "She's not there," I said.

"She's here," said Peter, and he touched my shoulder. The whale resurfaced, air blasting. Along her dorsal fin, the net clung in pale crisscrosses, like tracks or scars.

"I'll go first," he said.

"Have you done this before?"

His smile was sweet. "No."

"Peter!"

He went over the edge of the boat backwards, like scuba divers do. I peered over the edge. *Be careful!* She watched us intently.

Peter shook the wet hair out of his eyes.

"I'm coming in," I said.

"I don't think you—" he started, and I slid into the water.

Water covered me, but the cold didn't penetrate.

"How do you know what to do?" I asked.

"I've read about it."

We were treading water about ten feet from the whale. I wondered if she'd hurt us. How can you tell an animal that you won't hurt it, but want to help?

"Stay away from her flukes," said Peter. "Hopefully she'll just escape instead of attack. That's what I'm banking on."

I swallowed. She was huge—as long as a city bus. Much slimmer than a bus. Why couldn't the net have caught a small friendly dolphin? The story of Jonah kept popping into my thoughts. *God, please don't let the whale swallow me—or eat me or smash me*, I added for good measure.

"I'll try it first."

"Okay," I said. He swam slowly toward her head. Her mouth curved up in a small smile, not as wide as a bottle-nosed dolphin's smile. The net was under her throat and partially around her head and neck. Question: Do whales have necks? Not much.

About two feet away from her, Peter reached out his hand. She moved away. Peter tried again. I could hear him softly humming or murmuring to her. Like a dance, she mirrored his motions, but each time moved away.

He stopped a moment and we gazed at each other, prayers coming out of our eyes. He dived, and I watched underwater. He approached her from the side, and she moved just out of reach. I sighed underwater, round, firm bubbles coming out of my mouth.

When he came to the top, I said, "Let me try." I didn't know what I could do, but I took the pliers and swam to the whale. Peter moved aside. I dived, and the whale was looking at me out of one eye. The skin was wrinkled around it. How could I tell her I wanted to help her?

A school of fish veered around us. I surfaced and the whale did too, air rushing out of her blowhole. Was she imitating me, trying to be friendly?

Before I could touch her, she began to descend, every line of her body sagging. She turned her great eye from me. *No!* If she went down, I just knew she'd never come back up alive.

"Peter!" The boat's motor started and the chain groaned. He killed the engine over the whale and finished hauling up the anchor.

"Quick! Attach it to the net."

I seized it and dived. It was a traditional anchor, a straight bar with a curved bar. Both ends were fluked. The anchor pulled me down so it was easy to descend. My ears began to pop. The underside of the boat grew dim.

I swam after the whale, the anchor's chain unwinding behind me. She just kept shifting down, like she didn't care anymore.

But I cared. *We care!* My lungs were starting to burn. One hard kick and I stretched, the anchor light in my hands, to hook her. But she swerved. I missed.

My lungs burned more. If I went back up for air and she continued to sink, it would be too late.

Her body was a line of dark sorrow, bent. My ears throbbed so I swam over her, hoping she wouldn't suddenly rush up, because I didn't dare go deeper—how did someone get the bends?—and I wanted to surface alive.

I passed over her tail, her dorsal fin, then to the tangled net over her head. Reaching down, I snagged the anchor in the snarled mess. She thrashed. Bubbles roiled around us. She headed down, and I headed up. My lungs on fire. Black dots danced in front of my eyes. Almost there. Almost there. The surface was like a horizon. Was it getting closer?

I broke the surface, gasping. The breeze was ice over my face. Ah, air!

"Emily! You were down there so long! Are you all right?" Peter's worried face peered over the edge of the boat.

I could only nod, still heaving for air. The boat jerked. Peter unlocked the chain and fed the line out. He gave me a hand and hauled me in.

"I've only got a hundred feet," he said. I sat on the bottom of the boat, my heart hammering, but at least the air was easier to get down. The water was remarkably still for what was going on below.

"She'll tow us if she keeps going," I said, remembering Moby Dick too well.

"I was afraid she was dying, the way she was sinking," he said. "But I can always release the chain before she takes us for a ride."

The chain rattled against the boat's fiberglass hull, then quieted.

"I hope she didn't slip the chain," I said. I'd practically flung the anchor onto her.

"There's one way to tell." He tried to crank the winch. "Something's out there."

"What next?" I asked.

"I'm not sure. I'm making this up as we go." He swallowed, his hand on the winch. "I'm sorry I made you go down after her. It was dangerous."

"Don't worry about it," I said. "It made sense. I was near her already."

"Maybe we can try and coax her back up," he said. First he showed me how to start the small horsepower engine and to steer it with the rudder. I took a deep breath and thought I could do it. Dad had been showing me how to use the tractor at home.

Peter wound in all the slack chain and told me to go ahead. I started the engine and throttled it forward.

The boat jerked, like Dad's truck when the clutch popped.

"She's not drowned, is she?" I asked.

"I doubt it. Whales can hold their breath for an hour or so. Besides, if she were dead, she'd be pulling us with her."

That wasn't a very attractive thought. Suddenly the boat lurched backwards, and water rushed into the tipped stern. Whoa! The boat settled down, but my heart hammered in my throat.

Peter wound in more slack chain, and I kept the boat moving along. Water slopped around my feet.

"There she is!" he exclaimed.

She surfaced, the anchor on her back, hooked into the net. A blast of air split the sea, and she rolled on her side, her eye looking at us.

Steadily I drove the boat toward shore. It would be best to unhook her from the boat and tie her to the slip. Then we could work on her. She didn't dive, but swam with us, her flukes moving slowly.

Peter wound in the line. She resisted a few times, and the engine groaned, but she finally gave in and followed. Some pet. *Look, Mom. Look what followed me home*.

More of her showed as she grew closer. The glistening black body. The chalky saddle around her dorsal fin. She was handsome, even with the net clinging to her weird barnacles.

"Good girl," I called. "Almost there."

I cut the engine going into the slip and only bounced against one side of the edge. Peter leaped from the front and tossed the ropes in. We tied them fast. Then he busied himself with the end of the chain, securing it to the iron ring in the wooden slip. "I hope this works," he said. "I've never done this before."

"You haven't?" I teased. "Why I thought every kid

in See Canyon had towed a whale."

"Most everyone has. I'm a late bloomer."

"I see."

The whale gave a tug and the slip bobbed, seawater lapping up. In Psalms it talks about the ocean rejoicing, and the creatures of the deep dancing with joy. "Maybe we ought to pray," I said, feeling awed.

Peter gave me an amused smile. "We have got a tiger by the tail, haven't we?" He reached for my hand and pulled me out of the boat onto the slip. I started in, cutting to the basic: "God, please help us to free the whale. Make her be okay. Amen."

Peter added, "P.S. Please let the whale know we want to help her."

I was sure she knew that. She watched us out of her large eye. The slip bobbed again. Peter let out some chain, and I picked up the pliers.

As I turned to dive in, I saw people coming into the cove. Maybe someone would help. "Anybody know about gill nets?" I called.

People shook their heads, moms, surfers, a few dedicated-looking beach bums. Children crowded to the water's edge.

"Will someone call the Coast Guard?" asked Peter.

No one moved. Then a woman in shorts called back, "Someone already did."

Thank God. But there was no reason to wait. The whale needed help now, so I dived in.

8
Abalone

Waves closed over my head, green and mysterious, a world where humans were alien. I swam slowly to the whale. She knew I was there. Her big old eye was on me as she floated under the sea. The chain holding her to the boat trembled as she pulled back.

I surfaced. She rose to the top, her eye still on me. "Easy, easy there," I murmured and said silly things to her the way I do when Khan or one of the colts is scared. She remained still, letting the waves lap her body. Then fear snaked around me, tightening its coils like a sea serpent, making me feel I couldn't help the whale at all.

And to be realistic, she had power in those flukes. I had no doubt she could let me have it, and that would be it for Emily. Slowly I swam toward her round head. She opened her mouth, showing rows of teeth, and made funny squeaking noises, like chalk over a blackboard.

The reality of having a whale attached to a very small boat was, no pun intended, sinking in. Still talking to her, I reached out. She didn't recoil, so I touched her bulging head. She was cold. Firm. Like old marble. Then she shifted, and I drew back.

I went under and looked at her from the watery view. Of course she looked back and in those funny, wrinkled-looking eyes, I suddenly guessed at her world for a moment. Out of control. Insecure. Tangled up physically and mentally. (Do whales think?) Her circumstances not of her making.

Like me. I was bound, too, by things that I had no control over—like Mom, for one. But in the whale's case, at least I could free her from the net. I stroked her and she didn't pull back, but even pressed slightly against my hand.

With the pliers, I clipped the first line of netting. The pliers sprung it free and she jerked, the chain rattling into the boat. I moved closer to her head, as I did with colts. The closer you move to a horse, the less he can pack a kick against you. I hope this applied to whales, too.

After a few cuts, my hand began to ache. The net was tough. By cutting the net along her side, I hoped the net would slide off. It was snarled around her fins, so maybe I'd have to cut them out. Fortunately the net wasn't around her flukes, which were huge and undoubtedly felt worse than a double-hooved kick from a colt.

A blister formed on my hand. I thought the water might have acted as a lubricant. I kept cutting anyway, and my hand bled. I hoped there weren't sharks nearby.

Peter held onto the side of the boat, watching. He tried to come over to help, but the whale pulled back when he got too close. "The net tangles real easy," he called. "Be careful."

I *was* careful. Fortunately she remained near the surface, and I didn't have to hold my breath and cut underwater. I found if I braced my feet against her

77

firm skin and held on with my left hand, I didn't have to tread water. She let me hang on her.

She whistled softly, like a kid's toy. "It's okay," I said gently. "I'll get this thing off you."

Peter called, "How's it going?"

"She's being good," I called back. The wise eye stared at me, and I wondered if she knew what we were saying. It was uncanny to have a wild animal look you in the face so knowingly.

I worked my way up her dorsal fin, and she kept her body out of the water, so I didn't have to hold my breath and dive. As I got close to her dorsal fin, a black triangle, I saw that the anchor hooked into the gill net was cutting into her skin. She hadn't acted like she was in pain. Poor thing. The skin was pinkish around the gray patch. Carefully I unhooked the anchor and threw it away.

She rolled a bit, as if stretching, and I patted her. Then she moved away from me and dived straight down. The water boiled around me and splashed over my head. Coughing, I waited for the water to smooth over, then looked under the sea for her. She was gone.

"What happened?" asked Peter. He'd wound in the anchor line and swum out to me.

"Maybe she thought she was free," I said. "But she's not. That net is horrible."

About ten feet in front of us, the water shattered. The whale's dark form leaped from the sea, bursting above the waves with iridescent light. She breeched, full out of the water, and collapsed down on her back. A wall of water dashed us.

Peter sputtered. "Some show," he said.

The sea smoothed back down; only triangles of waves laughed towards the shore. Farther away from us, she rose again, her belly exposed, grayish white, and she leaped for the sun. She fell back with a splash.

Foam and water blew everywhere. She resurfaced near us and floated two arm's lengths away. *Well?* she seemed to say. *What's next?*

Peter swam back for another pair of pliers and I began to pinch the gill net strands around her fins. Some of the net had slid back in a crumbled mess like bedsheets, tangled after a nightmare. I knew about those, all right.

"Be easy," I told her, and she breathed at me, her blowhole exhaling sharply, loudly, the scent of old fish in the air. Steadily I cut through the hardy nylon-like stuff. My hand bled more. Peter swam up beside me, and this time the whale let him cut at the netting.

Finally my hand was so tired it barely would squeeze the plier handles. The gill net slid off her body, and I grabbed for it. I didn't want it ghost fishing for any other creatures.

"You're free," I whispered. She eased away, the waves carrying her. For a scary moment I thought she was sinking, but she suddenly turned her flukes to the sky and dived without a splash.

"That was terrific," said Peter, and I had to duck under the water to keep tears from sliding down my cheeks. *Dumb girl*, I thought. *Always crying.*

We swam back to the slip and climbed up. It took me a minute to find a solid foothold on the post to kick up, because my hand was useless.

"That was great, kids," said a voice. At first I thought it was Laing, but it was a man with a 35-millimeter camera and a note pad. He stepped onto the dock in his flaps.

"Hey, Mike," said Peter.

"Well, if it isn't Greg's son, stirring up trouble."

"Mike is from my dad's paper," Peter explained.

Behind Mike, a crowd of people still milled. Someone called to us, "Was that a shark?"

"This is a great story," said Mike.

"Didn't anyone call the Coast Guard?" I asked. "What if we hadn't been able to get this off her?" I kicked the net.

No one seemed to care about that, except Peter. He pressed his shoulder against mine.

"You two did a great job," said Mike cheerfully. "There was no need to. Someone called me, and now you'll get your reward. A great story in the paper."

"The only reward I want is to see the whale swim free forever," I said.

"There have got to be some better controls on gill netting," said Peter, and then Mike got into asking us questions. We told him the whole story, even about Khan rushing into the sea both times. He got all excited, kept running his hand through his hair until it spiked up from his scalp. He took photos of us.

"I want to see this horse," he said finally.

All during the interview, I kept looking out to sea, but the whale was gone.

We started up the path for Khan. All the people had left.

"Your father's going to be surprised," said Mike, as he panted behind us.

"I hope that's all he is."

"Won't he be proud that you helped save a whale?" I asked.

We reached the top of the bluff. I had to unzip my suit; it was too hot.

"He doesn't like attention drawn to our family. Status quo or something." Peter shrugged. "I can deal with him."

We showed Khan to Mike. She gave a long whinny, saying, *Where have you been?* Then she yawned right into Mike's camera. He probably got a great picture of her tonsils. After we hung up the wet suits, Peter and I swung up on her, and Mike snapped more pictures as we went back down the bluff trail.

Finally he left, and we sat on the dock, dangling our legs over the edge, Blues lying next to Peter. I held the reins with my good hand. Enough swimming out to sea for today.

"I wonder where she is," I said.

"I hope she's with her pod."

I hoped she was, too. But the selfish part of me wanted to see her again.

Our voices were silent for a while, and only the ocean spoke. Water rushing in and out. Slapping sparkling words against the rocks. The spray caught in the fading sunlight like trillions of tiny rainbows. Iridescent like the shatter of water when the whale broke the sea. Iridescent like the inside of an abalone shell.

"That's her name," I said suddenly.

Peter looked around. "Whose name is what?"

"The pilot whale. Her name is Abalone."

He grinned. "Are you sure?"

"Yes. Everything needs a name, because that makes it real."

"If something is unnamed, it's not real?"

"It makes that creature real to the other." I added, "God knows the names of the stars. He calls them by their names."

Peter gave me a crooked grin and reached for my hand. I recoiled, like the whale had. He pulled back, his eyes dark. "Sorry," he said shortly. "I didn't mean anything by it."

"No, it's just that I've hurt my hand."

"When?" He took my forearm and slowly I opened my fingers, but only partway because they were so sore. "I feel bad that I didn't even notice."

"That was the idea," I said. "It's just blisters on

81

blisters. That net was super tough."

"I know. It caught a whale."

For some reason that struck me funny and I started in laughing. Peter joined in, and we laughed for a long time.

Dusk fell in shifting layers, great strokes of dark orange and rippling lines of red. "The sea is glowing," I said.

"We'd better go."

"Yeah, I guess so." I wished we could stay all night, waiting for Abalone, to see if she were truly all right.

We rode back across the sands, my hurt hand in my lap. Peter's arms were tight around my waist. Beside us faithful Blues jogged, his tail up, his feathers waving.

Khan walked rapidly up the long hill to See Canyon, ignoring blinding car lights. One car slowed and I tensed, expecting a horn blast or a shout. People did that all the time, trying to scare the horses. Idiots.

Then a voice did shout. "Emily Sowers! Where have you been?"

Mom.

"Oh, no," said Peter in my ear.

"I was at the beach. It got later than I—"

"Go straight home. Now."

"But Khan—"

"Straight home after you put that animal away."

"Is she referring to me?" whispered Peter.

I stifled a hysterical giggle. The car window smoothly slid up, and Mom turned the car around, tires squealing, and roared up the hill. Khan snorted, and the exhaust made us all cough.

"I'm dead," I said.

"I'm sorry. I'll send beautiful flowers to the funeral."

"Thanks. I appreciate that."

The light from his house threw down beams that Khan neatly stepped over. When I turned her loose in the pasture, she immediately shoved her way between Seal and Mannie, flattening her ears at them until she got the best flakes of hay.

The night wind slid between Peter and me. How could I say anything to express what had happened on the sea? Uh, thanks for helping cut the whale loose? Thanks for being there? Everything sounded dumb.

We both started to speak at the same time, and then stopped. Instead, Peter touched my face with his hand.

"I'm glad we were there at the right time," I said.

"Me, too,"

I sensed a smile in his voice. It was too dark to see his face.

"Take care of that hand," he said and stepped back.

"I will."

"See you soon?"

"If Mom doesn't kill me."

"I'll be waiting." He bowed elegantly, like dancers do after a show, then left.

I wished I were on the sea with Abalone. Instead I was going home to mighty rough waves.

9
Dream Backwash

The porch light was on. When I stepped inside, Biscuit ran up and sniffed my leg as if reading the day's events. *You won't believe it*, I thought to him.

Mom and Jack sat at the table, the remains of dinner before them. Should I tell them? They'd find out soon enough, if the reporter really did the story.

Mom's mouth was tight and her eyes hard as marbles. "I've kept your food warm. Come and eat."

Silently I sat and glanced at the clock. Six-thirty. Was Abalone having a good meal? I hoped so. Mom slid a plate of creamed chicken, string beans, and salad under my nose. Then she and Jack drank iced tea and discussed whether they should reseed the back lawn and put in a hot tub.

I couldn't use my right hand, so awkwardly I lifted my fork with my left. Beans kept spilling off my fork. *Try to be cool*, I told myself, as a piece of chicken refused to be picked up. I didn't dare put my hurt hand above the table until I got a bandage on it.

Mom suddenly broke through Jack's talk as if she hadn't been listening to him at all. "Emily! What on earth did you do to your hand?"

Startled, I dropped my fork, and it bounced on the tile floor. Biscuit jumped up and licked the chicken from the prongs.

Mom seized my hand from under the tablecloth. "Open," she said.

I tried, but my muscles were too fatigued. "It looks worse than it is," I said. "Really. It's just a blister. No big deal." Except it was the size of my palm.

"Emily Sowers, how did you get a blister like that?"

I wasn't too good at lying. "From pliers. Peter and I were at the beach. He has this small motorboat."

"Did you have on a life preserver?"

"No, but I—"

"Honestly," snapped Mom, her nails clicking against the glass. "Don't you ever think? The ocean is dangerous."

I knew I had better not say what had happened today.

"Beth," Jack cut in, his voice a calming wind. "She wasn't alone. Peter and his sisters are half-fish. I've seen those kids in the sea since they were babies. Even the youngest, the one with problems, swims."

I wanted to ask what was wrong with Dawn, but Mom butted in, icily. "Thank you, Jack, but I can handle my own daughter."

His face tightened, and he got up and went into the living room. The television snapped on, and the tension fairly crackled. *My own daughter.* Like I belonged to her, like Biscuit.

I pulled my hand away. "I'm fine, Mom. Really. Don't worry."

She scooted her chair closer to me, her eyes changing from hard to soft, like a deer's. I had a sudden flash of insight as to why Dad might have fallen for her. His voice came into my mind: "Your mother is a beautiful woman. But beauty can be a trap. Remember that." I

85

remembered, but not because I'd ever be able to apply it to myself.

"What were you really doing, Emily?" she asked, a small smile slipping onto her lips.

I nearly smiled back. Mom could still read me, knowing I'd been up to something. I opened my mouth to tell her about Abalone, when she said softly, "You were with Peter, weren't you?"

"Of course I was with Peter." Then I stopped. That's not what she meant. She meant, You were *with* Peter. I got hot all over. "Mom, it was nothing like that. Peter and I hardly know each other. We were just—" and all the words that came to mind had double meanings. Fooling around. Messing around. Playing around. My face got hotter.

"Emily, at your age you need to go slowly and not rush things."

I couldn't help but think of Abalone. Don't rush things with the whale.

Then I got mad. She was accusing me of something I wouldn't do. I mean, really. I hadn't even had a proper first kiss. It wasn't fair. "Mom," I said sharply. "It wasn't like that at all. We were at the beach, and time got away. That was all."

"Okay, Emily." But I could tell she wasn't sure if she should believe me. Angry tears crowded to my eyes. Dad would have believed me.

"I'd never do anything like that," I said. "You don't know me anymore." I got up, and I was trembling.

"Well, I hope you wouldn't," she said. "Now go take care of that hand."

Upstairs I cleaned my hand. It stung, but the pain gave me something to focus on. After applying some topical medicine from the cupboard—probably not as good as our horse medicine—I wrapped it in gauze and figured I'd live.

The bathroom mirror had light bulbs around it, and I stared into my own eyes. What was Mom's problem? Why couldn't she just be glad I was here instead of trying to ride herd on me? I wished Melissa were here to talk to. Maybe I could call Dad, except Mom would probably get mad, thinking I wanted to go to him instead of her. Which was true. She'd hold it over my head and probably Dad's, too, saying something like: You're turning Emily against me.

Hardly, Mom. You're doing fine all by yourself.

Since I couldn't talk to Dad, I could talk to God, my heavenly Father. I knew that's what Melissa would say. She's very big on praying.

I sat on the bathroom floor—kneeling on tile hurts, so I hoped God would understand—with my feet up on the lower cupboards and my back against the other wall, and asked Him to please help me get along with Mom. Abalone played in my prayers, too. And Peter.

Later that night I dreamed. Or rather nightmared.

This time the scene of stars rapidly accelerated, like an incoming comet. I wasn't a star-baby this time, though, but a normal G-type star, burning in space.

The grinning face of death floated past the other stars who paled. I tried to slip from my body to get away, when the face swept by, heading for another star. Heading for my mother, an old, old star who'd never lived.

I woke in the darkness, grief pulsing my heart, and found that stars could cry, for all the stars wept for my mom.

The next morning everyone acted normal. Cool. No comments about last night. Jack chatted about a particular ranch house up for sale as I cooked breakfast. My hand didn't hurt so much this morning. When

Mom went upstairs for something, Jack said, "How's the hand?"

"Okay."

"Is this how you hurt it?" He held up the newspaper, and there in black and white were Peter, Khan, and I.

His manner was calm, but his words were a sudden scream. The bacon sizzled furiously. I didn't think Mike would have written the story so fast.

"Turn off the flame, Emily, before the grease explodes."

I did, and hastily lifted out the bacon with a fork and laid it on a paper towel. Then I sat down, and Jack handed me the section with the story. I read it fast. Mike made us sound more confident than I'd thought we had been, but he told what had happened simply. There was another photo of me cutting the net. I hated my picture. I looked ugly. Abalone looked pretty good. Dark, huge, like some monster.

Mom would have a cow if she saw this. "Can I keep this?" I asked him.

"Are you going to tell Beth?"

His eyes were soft, not pushing me, but I knew he'd tell her if I didn't. Duty and all that. I swallowed. "I'll tell her later. Tonight. I just don't want to have a fight at breakfast."

"Okay. Tonight."

I took the pages upstairs and shoved them under my bed. I wondered if Peter had seen it yet. Back downstairs I finished making breakfast and hoped no one in the office would pay attention to the story. At least my last name was different, and the photos of me weren't so great.

Mom came into the kitchen in a red and blue print skirt and blouse. I felt underdressed in my denim skirt and purple sweater.

I guess she thought so, too, because she said, "We'll go shopping today, Em, and get new clothes."

Dad had bought me this outfit for my birthday. I sizzled along with the bacon.

Jack said, "Don't forget she has that horse to train, Beth. Don't work her too hard."

I turned in surprise, and Mom laughed. "So the two of you are in cahoots, hmm?"

Jack merely winked at me.

"Okay," said Mom. "We'll be back in time for that infernal horse."

"She's not infernal. She's smart and loving."

"Sure. And I'm the Queen of England."

I set the plate before her. "Here's your breakfast, Queen." And we all laughed.

10
Inner Warmth

On the way to work, Mom and Jack chatted about real estate. I couldn't have cared less. We drove down the road to the ocean, but instead of turning right, off the highway, we went left and popped onto the 101 going north.

"There's the Madonna Inn," said Mom as we pulled off the 101 into San Luis Obispo. It was a pink monster rising off the rocky hills of bluish green serpentine stone. I disliked it immediately because it smacked of money and stupidness. And it was pink. I wasn't a pink girl.

"It's a beautiful place," said Mom. I sighed. The hills rose inside my soul as they were, not with a fancy hotel on them.

We pulled into a small office building near the Madonna Inn. Wind soaked with fog trembled through the parking lot.

Out of the Volvo, the winds swirled around me, heavy with moisture, but laughing, teasing. I braced my legs and let the wind come under my hair and blow at my skirt.

"Come on, Em," said Mom with a little smile. "The

winds never stop. You can play in them later."

She remembered. When I was little I used to run outside whenever the winds blew—and where we lived they didn't gust much. But how I loved the scent of wind and their fierce face. I still do. I trotted up to her, feeling like a frisky filly, and pushed open the heavy glass door with the gold block letters: Sea Breeze Real Estate. Inside a few people drifted around, except a receptionist who had a phone to her ear and was pressing lighted buttons. She handed pink slips to Mom and Jack and gave me a bright smile. She had eyes like a parrot's.

Mom introduced me to everyone. Jack and another man owned the business, so that made Mom high on the social ladder, I guess. The women cooed over me like I was a prize poodle or something.

"She looks a lot like you, Beth," said one woman, who stayed after the others had gone back to their desks. "She's pretty." Talking like I wasn't there. Besides, I know I'm not pretty, so she must have been trying to win points with Mom.

Mom showed me my work. Filing piles of papers. Copies. Duplicate copies. Totally boring. I wanted to set the duplicate copies on fire. But as I got into the swing of it, I began to plan Khan's training. I'd go to the library later and read up on it, but Dad and I condition colts all the time, so I knew some stuff.

Lots of hill work to develop the heart and lungs. Lots of trotting. I'd try some of that interval training and see how it worked. First, though, I needed to have Khan checked to see if she was in foal. I'd need to keep an eye on her off hind leg, but I thought it was sound.

"Lunch break," called Mom. I blinked and looked at the clock. Nearly twelve. Time flies when you're having fun, right?

Outside the winds had picked up, humming their ancient songs fast. I could hardly wait to get Khan and go.

We ate lunch at Burger King. Mom had a salad. I almost had a chocolate shake, but thought I better not. Khan wasn't the only one who was in training.

After lunch we stopped at one of the few big clothing stores in SLO. Mom insisted that I try on dresses and skirts. Finally we compromised on a dress, two skirts, and three blouses. I didn't look at the price tags. I hardly ever bought new clothes, except jeans and T-shirts, which go on sale pretty cheap.

I fingered the skirt, blue and green, loose and soft. It *was* pretty. "Thanks, Mom."

She looked pleased. "You're welcome." Then she turned me loose at the city library while she did some other shopping. "Half day today," she said and winked. "We'll ease you into the office."

"Thanks," I said again and was grateful for her flashes of insight or generosity or whatever it was. "I'm used to working outside. Being indoors makes me feel cooped up."

"I know." She kissed my forehead, not a fake kiss, but a gentle one like she did when I was home sick. "How like your father you are," she said. Then, before I could ask what she meant, she went on briskly. "I'll pick you up in two hours, okay?"

"Okay."

The wind curled after me like a playful pup. Question: Can you ever tame the wind enough to take it for a walk? That would be fun. A bit of the wind trotting at your heels.

The library door held the wind outside. *Wait for me*, I whispered to it. I didn't find any books on gill netting, so the librarian got me some magazines with articles about it.

Smiling, she handed me the magazines and said, "You're the girl who helped rescue the pilot whale, aren't you?"

I blushed totally red. I think even my back must have turned red. "Yeah," I said and couldn't think of another word to say.

"Good for you," she said, and I fled to a corner of the library with the magazines. Is this how celebrities feel? No, they like to be recognized. I was mortified.

As I read the articles, I realized how fortunate Abalone had been. Most animals caught incidentally drown before anyone can help them. *Thanks, God.* But then I tossed another prayer back at Him. *Why not make people stop using gill nets?* But I knew it wasn't that easy. People needed to catch fish to make money. And besides, we aren't robots. God lets us do pretty much what we want. And if people aren't careful with gill nets, then animals are caught.

Lots of whales were caught in the nets, not just pilot whales. (And I found in my reading that pilot whales weren't really whales at all, but big dolphins.) But humpbacks, killer whales, gray whales, southern right whales and lots more get caught in the nets.

I leaned back in my chair. We're talking big whales here. What if it had been a fin whale caught? It would have been the size of a two-story house—bigger.

After returning the magazines to the reference desk, I browsed for a long time and collected books on endurance riding and training. A girl not much older than me was paging books. Next to her was a cart piled high, and one book seized my attention. A Lipizzaner on the cover performed the *courbette*. That's where the horse rears and jumps, never letting his forefeet touch the ground. It's bizarre, but I love it. Nigel, a guy back home, is into the *haute école*, the airs of piaffe and passage, stuff like that. He's promised to teach me and Khan when school starts in the fall.

Also on the cover was a ballet dancer. A man. He was handsome, but the horse was more handsome.

"Can I check out this book?" I asked the girl.

She looked up. "Sure. Help yourself."

I flipped through it. It was big and heavy and had wonderful photos of the Lipizzaners and ballet dancers. At the checkout, I handed Mom's card to the clerk. It was all computerized, and she whisked the books through. As she wanded the dance book's bar code, she said impatiently, "I thought we'd gotten rid of all these old pockets. It even has the card in it still."

She started ripping out the pocket, and a name popped out at me. "Wait," I blurted. "May I see that?"

She gave me a weird look, but handed the torn pocket with card to me. Peter Kjaard's name was scrawled on it. Silently I handed it back. Peter was interested in the airs above ground? Common sense told me that he checked it out for one of his sisters, probably Cassie.

Mom was waiting out in front. On the way home she drove a different route. Toast brown hills skipped beside the car, lively, like calves, just like in the Bible. Blue serpentine rocks studded the hills' sides.

"This is the back way to See Canyon," said Mom, as we bounced over rough paved roads until we came to the top. Mom pulled over a moment. The town spilled behind us, and before us See Canyon, deeply wooded, cut down the swell of hills and poured out into the sea. Where was Abalone? I wished I had ESP, so I could communicate with her.

The engine purred on, and we plunged down the road, winding through the canyon, past farms and signs that read "organic apples for sale" and "organic honey for sale."

It sounded good. "Do you buy stuff here?"

She shook her head and gave me a look that said: Get serious. Never.

Excuse me. It didn't seem weird to me, but smart. I bet organic honey was good.

She let me off and drove back to the office with firm instructions, "Be back by six," and "Next time you'll stay at the office all day." I knew those things and nodded.

I changed, felt bad leaving Biscuit but had to, and ran to the pasture. I whistled for Khan. She grazed with the other two and ignored me.

"You beast," I told her and got out the bucket of oats Peter had left in the tack box. Khan instantly appeared, the others trailing in her wake. After grooming her, I longed her to be sure she trotted and cantered sound. She did.

"I'm impressed, Khan," I said. I was sore from all that swimming. Even though I'd wrapped my hand well, it throbbed.

Seal whinnied after us, but Khan left readily. She acted as if she enjoyed this country. As we reached See Canyon Road, I had every intention of turning up and exploring the unfurling hills, but my body didn't obey, and we headed once again for the sea.

We crossed the highway, and this time I clip-clopped Khan across the main street. People stared at us, and Khan began to prance.

"Show-off," I said and patted her neck. We turned our backs on the building, Khan prancing over the powdery sand.

Only a few surfers were out, and mothers were packing their kids up. I let Khan trot through the sand and canter on the harder packed wet sand. Avila

Beach wasn't very long. It ended at the great cliffs where the power company had towers. We could have gone around the beachhead, but Pirate's Cove was there. Mom had told me it was a nudist beach. I didn't want to see a bunch of naked people. Giving Khan a looser rein, we cantered back towards the pier. A bunch of guys walked near us, and I slowed Khan to move quietly around them when one called, "Hey, pretty girl."

The guys from yesterday. A sick pit spread in my stomach.

"Let's go, Khan." I jammed my heels in her ribs, and she lunged as the guy with stringy blond hair grabbed her headstall and held on. Khan grunted and stopped, confused, two humans telling her to do opposite things.

"Let my horse go," I demanded.

"I just want to talk to you."

Khan swung around, her nose pointing at him, her breath coming in hard squeals. She kept backing up, dragging the guy into the waves.

"I don't want to talk to you." I hit his hand with the end of my reins, but hit Khan, too, and she half reared. I didn't want her to dump me. Then I'd be super helpless. The guy's friends were laughing, but walking on. I hoped he'd go with them.

"You're something," he said. "You're really something up there on that horse."

"Yeah? You're really something, too—a creep!" I kicked at his arm. "Let go!"

He didn't, and I backed Khan up as fast as she'd go, her neck arched like an archer's bow, grunting under her breath. Waves splashed up her hind legs. Grimly I backed her farther. I'd drown before going anywhere with this guy. He just hung on, a credit to the mohair hackamore which didn't part.

I kicked again. His friends moved away, laughing, going down the beach. "Give me your phone number," he said. "Better yet, give me a kiss. I just want a kiss."

"No way!" I'd probably get the bubonic plague if I touched him.

The water swirled frothy. Khan stumbled and bobbed, her muzzle in the waves. She plunged up, squealing, getting mad. "Get him, Khan!" She flattened her ears and shoved at him with her face. She broke his grip, and he staggered backward. A wave broke over him and he went down, sputtering.

When he came up, he shouted and came for us, eyes furious. He grabbed my leg and yanked. I wrapped my arms around Khan. He'd have to pull my leg off. I wouldn't let go.

Khan jumped sideways, nearly unseating me. I tried to force her back under me, but I'd dropped the reins. An especially big wave dashed over us all. I choked, and my fingers slipped.

"Come here, baby," said the guy. "I won't hurt you."

"But you are hurting me." I kicked more, catching him once in the chin. I hoped it hurt. Suddenly he froze, and for a moment I thought I had hurt him, even knocked him out. He was staring past Khan, who'd turned her head and nickered.

The guy shrieked, "Shark!" and plunged through the waves for shore. Khan whinnied again, and I knew it wasn't a shark. It was Abalone.

The pilot whale raised her great head from the sea and chirruped. It was great. The guy ran from her.

Khan extended her head. The whale was too far out for them to touch, but Abalone made creaking sounds. Khan gave a low whinny. I longed to know what they said to each other.

Abalone vanished and resurfaced farther out, her flukes teasing the surface of the water. I wished I were brave and could just swim out there after her, but I was afraid to swim alone.

Khan moved willingly out of the water. "Not so hot to swim today?" I asked her. But today the whale wasn't hurt. Perhaps that had been Khan's reason for going out to sea.

Onshore I searched for the pilot whale, but she was gone. Fortunately those guys were gone, too. I grinned. Abalone had really scared him.

Then the wonder of it struck me. She had helped me. She had been watching out for me. That burst into a shivery glow inside me, and I rode home beaming.

11
Worth the Risk

I was freezing when I got home.

"What have you been doing, young lady?" asked Mom.

"Sort of fell in the ocean." Sort of, kind of, because of a whale, a horse, and a weird guy.

"With Peter?" she teased, but it wasn't funny.

"Not exactly."

After I'd showered and come back downstairs, combing through my hair which snarled worse than Khan's, I sat next to Jack in the living room.

"Something for you," he said and handed me a sheet of paper. An application for the Black Swan race.

"Thanks, Jack." I was impressed that he'd gotten this for me.

He ran his fingers through his graying hair. "Think you got a chance?"

I shrugged. It was an open race, which meant no categories or handicaps. I leaned back in the chair. Biscuit put his face onto my leg, and I stroked him. "Khan used to race, but she did terrible. But those were short races. Maybe she'll do better in a long race. Her endurance is already good."

"Arabians are like that. This'll be a long sprint, though."

The application listed the best winning time as nineteen minutes and four seconds. Black Swan had won the race in nineteen minutes and twenty seconds.

"I'll bet my money on you two," said Jack.

That was sweet of him. Was he trying to make points with me? If so, why? I gave myself a mental slap. *You're so suspicious, Emily. Give the guy a chance.*

Mom called us to a dinner of quiche (she'd even made the crust herself) and salad. Afterwards I cleaned up, knowing I needed to show Mom the newspaper article. Maybe I could just leave it on her bed.

No, that was the chicken way to do it. My dad always told us kids to be up front. Once when we had two colts in training, Red and Squirt, I saw what it meant to be up front. Red was the up-front colt. Smart, clever, and if he didn't like what you were doing he'd bite you. No problem. You'd slap his face or acknowledge you'd been wrong, and he'd forgive you.

But Squirt. He was sneaky and would kick you when he knew you weren't looking. Definitely uncool.

I did want to be upfront so, after wiping the counters and putting away the food, I went up to my room, got the article out from under my bed, and took it downstairs to Mom.

"This is what happened yesterday at the beach," I said. "And how I hurt my hand." I held out the article. She took it, not looking at it, but into my face. What did she see? Think? Then she read the article.

I sat on the couch arm while she read, chewing on my lip, missing my retainers because I like to chomp on them. Jack caught my eye once and winked.

Mom put down the clipping. A silly grin began over

100

my face. Just remembering Abalone and how she had helped me in return today.

"You were in the water with a whale?" Mom asked.

"Yeah." My grin faded. "She's a small whale." I remembered my library reading. "Actually, she's a large dolphin."

"Oh, that makes it better. My daughter is endangering her life with a small whale—no, only a large dolphin."

"Mom, my life wasn't in danger." Well, maybe a little. But important things are worth risks.

"And then the whole world reads this article and sees what a lousy mother I am, to let my daughter get into a dangerous situation."

"Now, Beth," Jack began, and she turned on him.

"You stay out of this. This is my daughter, and she has no business messing with a whale."

"It's not like she's a humpback whale or something. She's smaller than Khan," I said.

"Oh, well, I feel better now. Smaller than Khan. Always coming back to the horses."

Jack left, the front door shutting quietly.

I didn't dare tell her about seeing Abalone today. She'd really have a cow. "Mom, please. It's over, and I'm fine. I mean, Peter and I had to do something. We couldn't just leave the whale to drown."

But the look on her face said that we could have. That we should have. "Let me tell you something. A story," she said.

I sighed inwardly. I didn't want to hear little tales of woe or whatever, but I settled into the couch cushions, my feet drawn under me.

"I like animals, don't underrate me, but I know they can hurt you—kill you. When you and Ian were little, your father was thrown from a horse. I saw it from the kitchen window, and I covered your eyes and made

Ian take you to your room. I thought John was dead." Her voice swayed, then steadied. "I'll always remember the horse, too. A little buckskin. Skinny, ribs all over the place. He looked like a nothing colt, but he almost killed John."

I didn't remember anything about it. In fact, Dad had never mentioned an accident like that. "What happened to Dad?"

"Concussion. He was in the hospital for a week."

A glimmer of a memory slid into sight. A hospital corridor.

"I think I remember," I said, slowly. But I couldn't remember feeling any fear. Because I was too little? More likely because of Dad, who always said stuff like: "When something goes wrong between a horse and rider, it's usually the rider's fault. He needs to be smarter than the colt."

Mom sat staring up at the wall, smoking a cigarette. The smoke made me sneeze. "Sorry," she said and got up to open a window. Some of the smoke wafted outside.

"Mom," I said, trying to think out exactly what I meant. "Dad understands the risks with breaking colts. And I feel the same way. You just have to be careful." Of course, it was different with Abalone. It was more of a trust that she wouldn't hurt me. I didn't think I could explain it to Mom.

"That's the heart of the problem," said Mom. She snuffed out the cigarette. "Nothing is worth the risk of getting hurt."

How could I explain that if you love something enough or know something is right, you do it, regardless of the risk? It was like becoming a Christian, in a funny sort of way. When Ian first told me about Jesus, I felt like he'd opened a door into another world. I had to decide to step into that world. Take a risk.

"Well, the whale is gone, most likely," I said. "Off with her pod somewhere." Away from ghost fishing nets, I hoped.

"I won't forbid you to go to the beach, but leave that whale alone. I think I'll call some people tomorrow. Can whales get rabies?"

"Mom! Anyway, she didn't even scratch me."

She pointed at my gauze-wrapped hand.

"That was from the pliers. They weren't even rusty. So I won't get lockjaw. Or rabies. Or barnacles."

"Barnacles?"

"Or anything."

A slight smile crossed her face. "Okay, Em."

I got up to leave, and she said quietly, "One other thing. I tried to love your father's work, but I couldn't. But that doesn't make me abnormal or evil. I'm just different. Will you grant me that?"

That wasn't too difficult, but what made tiny tears creep to my eyes was the thought, *Did you ever love my dad?*

The rest of the week slid by. The veterinarian, Dr. Myers, came out in a white truck and checked Khan on Saturday. I haltered her and held her outside the pasture. Seal and Mannie stared jealously at us, certain Khan was getting a special treat.

"A race mare?" asked Dr. Myers, running his hands over Khan's neck, her shoulders, down her legs. I felt like saying, *The foal should be near her rump.*

"She once was," I said. "I'm planning to enter her in the Black Swan race."

He pulled on a thin glove and put his hand into her rectum. Khan clamped her tail and squealed. I jerked on the lead line. Maybe I should have put a twitch on her. "Behave," I said, but I didn't blame her one bit.

"She's all right," said Dr. Myers. "As long as she

only makes noise. It's the kicking I don't appreciate." His whole arm was in her, and he looked up at the sky while he felt for the foal. I imagined it floating like a sea horse, playing hide and seek with him.

"When was she bred?"

"Six weeks ago."

"Has she come back into heat?"

"I'm not sure. She has silent heats. It's really hard to tell unless there's a stallion around."

He felt around some more. Khan's ears were pinned back. When he pulled his hand out of her, she aimed a kick. He dodged.

"Khan!" I snapped the lead line hard. She looked pleased.

Dr. Myers peeled off his glove and stuffed it into a bag in his truck. "Lots of mares try that."

Opening the pasture gate, I led her through, took off her halter and sent her away. She squealed and broke into a trot, then a full-fledged gallop, bucking and twisting.

"I don't think she's in foal. We could bring her into the clinic and do ultrasound to be sure, but I don't think she is."

I sighed. I'd so hoped she'd have a foal. I'd have to wait until the fall to have her rebred.

"What if she really were pregnant, would it hurt her to race?"

"The Black Swan race? I doubt it would."

Dr. Myers rearranged equipment in his truck as I counted out the bills. Mom had cashed a check for me. He took the money. "Thanks. See you at the race. I'm an on-call vet there."

After he'd gone, I sat on a bluish-green rock in the middle of the pasture. On a lined notebook page, I began creating Khan's training schedule. Walking to warm up. Trotting up hills. Some jogging through the sand, but not too much. It's a strain on the legs.

The horses drifted around me, grazing, ears flickering, tails sounding like brooms sweeping.

Closing my eyes, I could imagine riding Khan in the race, winning, lengths in front of everyone. My practical voice said, *Get real, Em. If you manage to win by some quirk, it won't be by lengths*. If only I could think of some extra training method that would make the difference. *Dream on!* said my practical voice. So I did. Khan on the beach. Abalone there and Peter. Khan swimming, me clinging to her back.

Swimming. It was supposed to be the perfect sport, because there was almost no concussion. Suppose I swam Khan a lot? Maybe that would be the edge we needed.

And to be honest, it gave me a legitimate excuse to look for Abalone.

I put my head up. What I needed now was a legitimate excuse to see Peter. I hadn't seen him in three days. I couldn't think of any reason to go to the door and ask for him. I guess I could just be honest: "Is Peter there?" And invite him to come with me to the beach. Why not?

But I didn't. I was too chicken. Maybe he thought I had the plague or something.

I rode Khan in the hills, and both of us chased out bad feelings while galloping along the hillsides.

12
Fluid Motion

That night, while I was writing letters to Melissa and to my dad and brothers, the phone rang.

"For you, Em," said Mom.

I took it in the kitchen. "Hello?"

"Hi, this is Peter. How's your hand?"

It was good to hear his voice. I twirled the phone cord. "Fine. Healing pretty fast." Then in a rush I said, "I've got something really great to tell you about Abalone." I dropped my voice on her name, but the television blared over me. "But I can't tell you right now."

"Can you come over to the pasture?"

I looked at the kitchen clock. Seven-thirty. "I'll ask." I put the phone down. "Can I run over to see Khan and talk to Peter for a few minutes?"

"I suppose," said Mom.

"See you there in a few minutes."

Grabbing my sweatshirt and a carrot for Khan, I merged into the night and ran for the pasture.

Peter stood in the grass, the horses surrounding him.

"Hey," I said.

"That was quick."

"I ran." Khan, the greedy gut, snuffled over to me and neatly took the carrot.

"What's up?" he asked and sat on the big rock.

"I saw her again. Abalone." I told him what had happened. At the mention of the guy harassing me, his face darkened, but when I told him about Abalone appearing, his face lightened, laughing.

The exhilaration of being with her rushed through me, like when I drink too much caffeine. She'd saved me from that guy!

"I wish I'd been there. I would have loved seeing that guy run."

I didn't know what else to say. I've always hated girls that chattered constantly, so I kept my mouth shut and stroked Khan, straightening her mane.

The night passed quietly between us. Peter had lounged back against the rock. Finally he said, "I called to see how you were, and also to see if you wanted to go to church with us in the morning."

I'd been wondering what I was going to do about church. I wasn't convinced Mom would drive me. I'd thought about riding Khan, but this would be much less complicated. "I'd love to," I said.

More silence went between us, and I knew I ought to be getting home. "I was at the library," I said, "looking at stuff about pilot whales and gill nets and endurance training, and I saw this one book. It had horses and a dancer on the cover, and you'd checked it out."

I thought he'd be mildly interested or basically unconcerned, but his whole body went rigid. The pale light from the house fell over him in harsh lines, as if he were stone.

Then I thought perhaps he was sick. "Peter," I started.

He sat up. The hard lines slid away, and he became

a guy on a rock again. "A book about dancing horses?" he asked, his voice too casual, too light.

"Yeah. Are you into airs above ground?"

For a moment I thought he was going to say something—well, I wasn't sure. Something important. Something that explained the odd things he did. But he only said, "I don't remember anything like that. Maybe Cassie had my card."

But it was your signature. I almost explained about the old checkout system just to let him know I knew he was lying, but then I figured it wasn't worth a fight. Maybe I was just imagining crazy things. Who knew? Maybe Cassie could forge his name.

"Well, I'd better go home." I gave Khan a final pat.

Peter got up. "See you tomorrow morning."

I watched him leave, pretending I was messing with my shoes. He moved in the pale moonlight just like the dancers in that book. Fluid motion.

Oh, well. He was strange, but I still liked him. I hiked home, skipping over the fallen branches and pretending like I used to that I was a horse.

At eight-thirty a.m. I was back at the pasture, then up to the house where everyone was getting into the station wagon. The pasture was awash with pink and gold. It was a new country, compared with last night's pasture.

Peter's whole family was there, and I was nervous. But when Peter saw me walking up the path, he ran lightly down to me.

He looked really great. Almost the kind of guy you'd imagine in a fashion magazine. Not that I drooled over guys in magazines, but with him I might.

"So this is the famous whale rescuer," called a man who I figured was Mr. Kjaard. Taller than Peter by a head, with the same curly blond hair.

"She did all the work," said Peter.

"Not quite," I said and wanted to kick him, but didn't. I could imagine my mom saying, "You do not kick men while you are wearing a dress."

Peter and I climbed in. Dawn, in her car seat, was between us. Cassie and Abigail, the oldest, sat in the far back. All blonde. They all looked like they belonged in the Swiss Alps or along some fjord somewhere.

"Where do you go to church at home?" asked Mrs. Kjaard.

I told her. She said, "Our church is a little different. We meet at a Grange Hall."

"What's that?" I hoped it wasn't some weird cult.

"It's a club like a Lions' Club. We just rent the building on Sundays. That way we don't have to worry about keeping up a church and yard."

That made sense. Dawn gave me a big, unexpected grin and said, "Eee."

"That's right," I told her. Peter looked pleased.

The church wasn't a cult. The music started as we filed in. Just a piano. The whole service was like that. A simple line of music running through the souls of the hundred and fifty or so people there. It was like home except for one thing. All the kids stood, even little kids, and recited a Scripture verse from memory.

I sat wondering if they expected me to say a verse. The one I knew best was Job 39 about the horse. Next to me Peter stood and said his verse in confident tones. Then he sat, and I stood and said my verse.

When I sat back down, Peter whispered, "You didn't have to. We hadn't even warned you."

"I wanted to do it," I said. And in some fierce way I had. I wanted to be a part of these Christians because I missed the casual talking I did at home about the Lord. My mom's house was like a foreign country where my mother tongue wasn't spoken.

We bowed our heads for the last prayer, and Cassie took my one hand and Peter took the other. I hoped my palms weren't sweating too much. He didn't seem to notice. Or maybe it was his palms that were doing the sweating.

The Kjaards dropped me off in front of the house. I told them thanks, but that was an understatement. It was as if they'd cut away some lines of net that had been wrapped around me. I could move better after being with Christians.

The rest of the day sorted itself by. I read, wrote letters, and leafed through the oversized book with page after page of horses and dancers. What was Peter's secret? Or was there one? Mom used to tell me I had an overactive imagination.

Working at Sea Breeze Real Estate got a tiny bit easier. I worked all day Mondays and Fridays and usually half days on Wednesday. My favorite part (other than leaving) was to canvass. I like walking through San Luis Obispo, delivering handbills and seeing the old Victorian houses on Marsh and Broad Streets. Some of the people were fun, and even though I did mostly filing and super boring clerical work, it gave me time to plan training schedules for Khan, pray, and think more and more about Peter.

The way he'd held my hand in church (*don't get so heated up, Em; he was holding his sister's hand, too*). The way we helped Abalone together. My brain jumbled with images of Khan, Abalone, and Peter, and often not in that order.

The Fourth of July swept up suddenly like an undertow. It always does somehow, like it ought to be later in the summer. We had a picnic at the beach with some friends of Mom and Jack's and watched the fireworks shot off at the end of the pier at Avila. I wondered about Abalone. Did the fireworks scare her? But my practical self said sternly, "She's gone with her pod. That's what's best for her." *Yes, I know, but that can't stop my selfish self, who wants to see her just one more time.*

Peter called about a week after the Fourth. "Doing anything tomorrow?"

"Just riding Khan."

"I have the day free," he said. I wanted to ask, *Free from what?* but he kept talking. "Do you want to have a practice race with Seal?"

"That would be great."

"See you at the pasture."

That night I dreamed, or rather nightmared, in the true sense of the word. I dreamed Khan was having a foal, but a horrible, mishaped foal. Awful.

I tossed and turned under the covers, and like those horrid movies where the human transfigures into a werewolf, I felt my body changing into a baby star.

Not again.

Suddenly I sat up, awake. Someone had spoken to me. Then, as I straightened my twisted nightgown, I realized I'd spoken and wakened myself.

I lay back down, relieved that I didn't have to go into space and see my mom dying, the wicked face (not much in the world deserves to be called wicked, but that face did) and I struggling to live.

The moon was gone. Outside my window, stars gleamed, polished by the wind. I thought of Peter, asleep in his bed. Maybe he slept like Farley, arms flung wide, belly down like a kitten. Or maybe like Ian, who sometimes still fell off his narrow bed at night.

My heart started thudding, thinking of Peter, and I

realized I'd been dreaming before the nightmares, dreaming of Peter, being out in his boat, his arms around me, rocking on the sea.

Even in the dark, with no one around, my face turned hot. I buried my face under the cool pillow and closed my eyes.

The next morning I ran for the pasture. Coming up through the snarled blackberry vines, I saw Peter with the horses, and my face turned hot again, thinking of my dreams. I stopped.

He must have heard me, because he waved, and then I had to keep going, climbing through the barbed wire and trampling down the dew-soaked grass.

"Hey," he called. "How are you?"

"Fine." I felt stupid, not knowing what to say. If he asked what was wrong, I wouldn't be able to tell him. Khan cruised up on my right and pulled a carrot from my back pocket.

"How's your hand?" asked Peter. He insisted on inspecting my palm. It was practically all healed.

"I almost wish it would scar," I said. "Then I could tell people I was blood brothers with a pilot whale."

He'd already groomed Khan and held out her hackamore to me. I knotted it around her face, and she chewed the carrot contentedly.

"Ready?" he asked, and we rode out of the pasture. Mannie whinnied after us, but Seal didn't even answer. His long whiskers only quivered smugly. "We can ride this trail. It's just about five miles. We clocked it once, because I used to jog it." He rode bareback, too, and rode well, despite Seal's prancing and bouncing.

The trail veered off from the side of the road and ducked into a valley of hills. "Let's go."

And we were off, the horses cantering side by side,

Seal stretched out a little more because Khan took such long strides.

Peter's shirt was a pale blue and red, and in faint letters across the back it read *Joffrey Ballet*. All of a sudden I knew. I knew his secret. It all came together with a click. His grace. His muscles. Even his vanishing acts. He was involved in dancing. But why didn't he just tell me?

I almost blurted it out, but I didn't. If he wanted to tell me or never mention it, that was up to him. I wasn't going to force him. We do that with colts. Dad refuses to rough up a horse and force him to cooperate. We're just there, and they soon come to us to be friends.

So I concentrated on racing.

The trail began to narrow, and Seal clung to the lead, mostly because I hadn't been paying attention. Khan breathed over the pony's rump.

The miles clicked by. Next time I'd bring a watch to clock her. Seal picked up his pace, straining, and Khan easily stayed right on his tail.

"Five miles is at the cluster of trees," shouted Peter. They were about a quarter of a mile away. Seal and Khan thundered along. Khan's shoulders were sweaty, and my thighs and shorts were wet.

She could go faster if Seal wasn't in her way, so carefully I guided Khan off the trail and onto the rougher ground. She flew alongside Peter and Seal. Peter yelled and leaned over the pony's neck. Seal flattened his ears, but Khan surged by, gained the lead, and crossed back in front.

We galloped past the trees first.

"You won," I whispered in her twitching ear. "You're a winner."

She didn't act impressed, only jibbed her head and tried to break out of the trot I held her down in.

"That was great," exclaimed Peter, his face alight. His eyes had that sea light in them. "I bet you'll do really well."

"I hope so. Do you think it's fair to pray to win?"

He gave me a funny, sideways smile, as if he'd thought about that before. "I think it's better to pray to do your best. Sometimes doing your best is better than winning."

"That sounds so noble," I said as we walked the horses to cool them down. Tendrils of wind curled around us. Whenever we passed bunches of oak trees, birds' songs tumbled through the air. "I guess I had this idea that prayers sort of cancel each other out. I mean, what if two Christians pray to win? I thought maybe it was like voting or something."

"I know what you mean. It's weird to think about prayer. I used to wish it was like a magic spell. I could cast it, and it would work."

"But it doesn't."

"Not like that."

I rode along, wondering why things that seemed good, like my mom getting saved, like no more gill nets, babies not deformed, didn't happen. Why? But sometimes good things did happen. Like Khan. I patted her drying neck. Like meeting Peter. Helping Abalone.

"I think," said Peter, twirling the ends of the reins, "that prayer is like a beautiful dance. Have you ever gone to the ballet?" He looked me in the eye, like he was gauging my response as well as explaining something.

I shook my head.

"It all works together. The music. The dancers. The whole set. Even the audience, because the more appreciative they are, the better the dancers do."

I couldn't help but smile—it was so different.

He gave me a dark look that crushed me. "Never mind," he muttered and looked down at the trail Seal walked.

"Peter, I didn't mean anything except that it sounds pretty. It's just different. I mean, my Sunday school teacher doesn't say stuff like that."

He looked back at me, his eyes softer. "Okay, sorry. I'm just touchy."

I know. But I didn't say anything except quietly, "It's okay." Because it was.

We climbed the hill to Laing's. As we crested the cliff, the sea scent curled over the top and dashed our faces. Khan's mane blew straight out, like torn flags.

Laing was working on his truck outside the house, near the shed. A metal box of tools was at his feet, and a big orange cat sat in the open toolbox, on top of the pliers and wrenches, licking its shoulder.

We stopped the horses. The cat gave us a level stare, and Laing pulled his head out of the engine area.

"Hi, kids," he said. Then, after glancing between us, he said, "So let the cat out of the bag. No offense, Kit," he told the orange tom.

"What?" Peter looked startled, and I laughed at them both.

"I know you two are up to something," he said. "So out with it."

We grinned at each other. We hadn't talked about Laing helping us with Abalone, but I think we both knew he might.

"Did you read about the pilot whale caught in a gill net?" began Peter.

"Did I ever." Laing hoisted himself onto the truck hood and said, "Tell me what happened."

So Peter told him about Abalone, and then I told him about Abalone chasing off the guy.

The orange tomcat jumped up on Laing and sat purring in his lap. "I'm an old squid," Laing said, "but I've never heard anything like that."

"That guy'll think twice about bothering girls again," said Peter.

"Consider yourself warned," I said.

Laing laughed, and Peter gave me a shocked look. "Emily, I thought you liked me."

"Just watch your step, or Abalone'll be after you." If we ever saw her again. It had been two weeks.

"See, this is the problem," I said. "We're afraid she'll get tangled up again. And my mom hasn't quite forbidden me to go near her. Isn't there some way to show her pilot whales are harmless?"

Laing petted the cat silently. Peter slid off Seal and turned the pony loose to graze. I didn't dare do that with Khan, so I stayed on her, but let her put her head down to graze the short grass.

When Laing looked up again, his lips were pressed together and he shook his head. "Pilot whales, any marine mammal, can be dangerous."

I groaned. "Don't tell me that."

He ran a hand through his wild hair. I wondered: Does he ever brush it?

"This is difficult," said Laing. He looked over at Peter, who sat in the grass, his long legs out in front of him. "I've got what I want staring me in the face, but I can't do anything about it."

"What are you talking about?" asked Peter.

"I've always wanted to do research on marine mammals, especially whales and dolphins. A lot of us marine biologists do, but it's nearly impossible to make friends with them. Unless you capture them."

"Poor things," I said. "They deserve to be free."

Peter said, "Here comes Emily, who isn't even from our beach, and she makes friends with Abalone."

"That's right," said Laing. "It's ironic. It's very wonderful, too."

I didn't understand why they spoke so despairingly, like it was a sad thing. "I'll do research with you," I said eagerly. "Then my mom will have to let me work with Abalone." For the sake of science—she'd have to.

"I haven't got the money or the time," said Laing. "I wish I did."

"If Khan wins that race . . ." I began and trailed off, thinking that sounded sort of dumb.

"Thanks, honey, but it would take thousands of dollars to do a proper research. Besides, do you even know she's around anymore?"

Peter and I looked over at each other and shook our heads.

"I hate sounding like the damper on your fun, but she's probably returned to her pod, and they're hundreds of miles away," said Laing.

My mind knew that was true, but my heart didn't believe it. I sighed. Last year I'd had a crush on this guy who didn't know I existed, and he shattered my heart. Now my heart was shattering again, this time from the loss of a whale. Or did I ever have her? No, I didn't. Not truly.

"Sorry, kids," said Laing. Peter stood up.

"Thanks anyhow. I wished you'd been there," he said. "I was scared."

Laing's eyes sparkled. "So it was Emily who saved the day."

"Hardly," I protested. "Besides, I was terrified, too."

"That's true courage. Doing something even when you're scared." Laing winked at me.

I wanted to throw my arms around his neck, because he was understanding. He listened. Unlike my mom, who just talked at me. Instead, I guided Khan up to him and held out my hand. Gravely we shook. His palm was calloused and rough.

Peter caught Seal, and we rode down to the beach. I tried to get Khan to swim, as I'd been thinking about, to exercise her, but she refused to go any farther than chest deep.

"Next time we come, we'll get in the boat and force her out," said Peter.

Silly mare.

We rode around in the hills and came home just in time for dinner.

For a moment, when I stood next to Khan in the pasture, I thought Peter was going to touch me, draw me to him, but he didn't. My mind burned with the image of my dream. Peter and I. I wanted him to hold me. To kiss me. Instead we parted and I walked home, wishing for my retainers to chomp on.

He still hadn't told me he was a dancer. Maybe he really wasn't—no, he was. I just knew it. I wished he'd confide in me. Tell me what was going on.

How could I be fifteen and still feel like I hardly knew anything?

I rubbed my head and walked into the house. I hoped tonight would be cool, calm.

But of course it wasn't.

13
Peter's World

After dinner Mom and I sat outside on the back porch. Jack was working late, showing properties up in Atascadero. I read the endurance books, leaning back in the hard plastic chair, my feet on the edge of a huge brown ceramic pot holding a three-foot star pine.

Biscuit snored at Mom's feet. She stared up at the changing sky, an unlit cigarette between her fingers. "You know, Em," she said, "we could use you another day in the office."

Two and a half days were already too much! "I'm pretty busy trying to get Khan ready for this race," I said.

She gave an impatient sigh. "Horses aren't the whole world. You need to stop living in such a dream world."

"It's not a dream world." *It's more solid than houses and money.*

Mom lit the cigarette, and the smoke curled up through her silvering hair. "Emily, I just don't want you to be trapped like John is."

"Dad's not trapped."

"All he has are the horses. The horses this. The horses that. You kids used to do without, so the horses could be fed," she said. "It's ridiculous, and I won't have it for you."

I didn't remember ever doing without—except doing without a mom. "Dad loves us more than the horses. You're exaggerating. Maybe he was like that before he was a Christian, but he's doing great *now*."

She didn't answer. I wished I could see into her thoughts.

"What has your father said about us breaking up?"

I clutched my fingers around the book. "He doesn't have to say anything. I saw what happened."

"And what did you see?"

My thoughts tumbled back two years—even earlier. Flashes of images careened in my head, like spooked horses. Their fighting in low tones, so as not to wake us kids. Arguing because there wasn't money to pay bills. Just the current of life, love lost in the rapids, and all that was left was an empty shore. "You left Dad for Jack," I said. "You stopped loving Dad."

She tapped her pale purple nails against the armrest of the chair. "John has you brainwashed, doesn't he?"

"No."

"I didn't even meet Jack until six months after I left."

But it was you who left.

"And it's true, I filed for divorce—because your father was so wrapped up in the horses that he couldn't do it himself. Let me tell you something, missy, your father isn't a prince like you seem to think."

Anger washed through me. She thought she knew so much about Dad, me, life. She didn't know anything.

"You stop talking down Dad," I said in a tight voice. "Just remember, you left us. You left us!" And I jumped up, hating myself for running, but I had to get away because the net was tightening around me. I knew how Abalone must have felt. I ran out of the house.

The moon, a silver curve above, burned into the darkness. I wanted to reach up and touch its healing fire, to burn out my own anger. But it just didn't work that way.

The horses grazed peacefully, Khan between the other two. To go to them would intrude. Besides, as much as I loved Khan, I wanted human friendship.

So I knocked on the Kjaards' front door, praying like mad that Peter would open the door.

He didn't, but Mrs. Kjaard, with Dawn on her hip, did.

"Emily, come in."

"Is Peter here?"

"Not yet, but he will be soon. Will you wait?"

I didn't want to go home. "Is it okay?"

"Of course. In fact, I could use your help. How's that?"

"Sure." What a relief. Nothing was worse than sitting around, trying to make conversation. I followed her into the kitchen.

Every Sunday I'd gone to church with them, but I met them at the car or they picked me up at home, so I'd never seen the house before.

The kitchen looked Danish or something. Blue and white dishes sat in a glass case. On the wall hung large, glass-framed photos of a wild, mountainy country.

Mrs. Kjaard held Dawn out to me. "She's been wanting someone to hold her all the time. It's hard to get things done."

Dawn stared crossly at me out of her funny, slanted eyes. Mrs. Kjaard opened the oven door and pulled out a cookie sheet of chocolate chip cookies. As they cooled, she began rinsing off dishes.

"Hos," said Dawn in my face.

"That's right. Khan's my horse." I rocked back and forth, and Dawn laid her head on my shoulder. When Farley was little, I used to carry him around. I'd never played with dolls as a child, but I loved baby Farley. I wanted to take him everywhere, even to school.

"Peter speaks of you often," said Mrs. Kjaard. "I'm glad you two are friends—he needs some good friends. These last few years have been hard on him. He's rather caught between two worlds."

So Peter talked about me. My face grew warm at the thought. I almost asked Mrs. Kjaard if Peter was a dancer, but I still wanted him to tell me. I didn't want to play detective.

Dawn gurgled in my ear and wrapped her legs around my waist.

"You've found a friend," said Mrs. Kjaard. "Dawn doesn't often like people outside the family."

Little children and whales follow me around. I smiled at Dawn, who said, "Pee pee," as the front door opened, bringing in Abby and Peter.

"Dad's working late," announced Abby, tossing back long blonde hair that I would kill for. "Cassie's staying with him because it's something about a demonstration at the nuclear plant."

"I can't imagine why a ten-year-old is so fascinated with political issues," said Mrs. Kjaard.

"She'll be president one day," said Abby carelessly, grabbing a cookie.

For those moments Peter hadn't seen me, standing beside the coffeepot, Dawn on my hip. His eyes had bags under them. He set a gym bag down on the floor. A blue towel was around his neck, and he had on black tights and a leotard.

"Em's here to see you, Pete," said Mrs. Kjaard, taking the little girl from me.

The tiredness fell from his face, and he smiled. Then his eyes clouded over and he glanced down at himself. *She knows.* His thoughts were stones thrown. But why is it a fearful thing?

Abby slapped Peter on the back. "This boy works too hard. Slow him down, Em, okay?"

Peter made a face at her. "Want to go downstairs?" he asked.

I followed. What was downstairs? I stifled one of my hysterical giggles while imagining a dungeon below. A rack. Rotating knives. I was as weird as my older brother.

Peter flicked on a switch, and the room lit up. Mirrors blazed back from the far side of the wall, and a *barre* ran the length of the converted basement. He sat down on the exercise mat and patted the space next to him. I sat, and he stretched his legs out and touched his head to his knees—something I doubted I could do.

I wanted to say something to him, like, *I caught you.* But I didn't. Silently I watched him stretch out.

"Quiet, aren't you?" he said and lifted his head. His hair was damp and even curlier than usual.

"How long have you been a dancer?" I asked.

He put his hands behind him and rested back on his arms. "For years." He looked at me closely. What did he see? "Surprised?"

I shook my head. "I guessed it."

A half smile touched his lips, then he said quietly, "A lot of people, especially those I'm close to, think I should give up dancing. I didn't tell you at first, because I liked you too much to risk finding out that you thought what I did was stupid."

"I don't think it's stupid."

He looked at me. "Thanks." Then he pulled his legs under him and said, "So, what's up? You're acting funny, and it's not because of my dancing, is it?"

I shook my head again. "Big fight with my mom."

"I'm sorry."

"It's not your fault."

"I know, but I'm still sorry."

"She was trying to tell me that my dad's a jerk," I said. "It's not true. If anyone's a jerk, it's Mom."

He stretched some more on the mat. I tried to imagine him dancing. "What do you do? Ballet?"

"And jazz. I've done two rock videos," he added.

"Are you serious? Which ones?" Dad only let us watch MTV when he was there—to monitor our viewing habits, as he said.

Peter told me the names, and I thought I remembered them, but I didn't remember Peter.

"I was in with a bunch of people," he said. "It wasn't like a solo or anything. With the money I earned, I bought *The Sparkle.*"

"How great. I wish I could see them."

"I just happen to have copies," he said and grinned.

"I want to see them!"

"They're packed away. I'll dig them out later. So, tell me more about your mom."

As I talked, he stretched and did these funny squats, knees bent, one hand on the *barre.* "Plies," he explained at my puzzlement. "Didn't you ever take ballet lessons?"

"Only the horses."

"You're as obsessed as I am."

I told him about my dreams, my nightmares of the brown dwarf. He didn't know that stars had a life cycle and came and knelt before me, listening as I explained about baby stars, red giants, and how our star was middle-aged and ordinary.

When I'd finished he sat quietly, the tiredness back in his face. I began to get up. "I should go," I said. "You need to rest."

"No, not yet." He caught my hand and pulled me back down. With a fluid move, he put his arms around me and pulled me to him. His hair crinkled under my face, and I touched his face. "You feel different from Abalone," I said, and he burst out laughing.

"I'm not a whale."

I laughed, too. "You're softer than Khan."

"I'm not sure I like being compared to the animals."

Still laughing, I said quickly, "But you're much nicer than they are."

"That's a relief."

He held me again and this time kissed me. My first kiss. Fireworks should have gone off, but instead I was assaulted by a warm feeling in my stomach. His lips were soft. Funny. I wouldn't have thought a boy would be so soft. I wanted him to kiss me again, but he didn't.

"It's nearly ten," he said. "I'll walk you home."

The moonlight was muted in the fog. "Want to go to the beach tomorrow?" he asked. "I'm free until the late afternoon."

"Sure." I hoped Mom didn't mean she wanted me to start working an extra day right away. "Do you think we could try swimming Khan from the boat?"

"Yeah."

At my door, I thought he'd kiss me again, but he stepped back and gave me a funny bow. He was still in his dance tights and leotard, so he looked perfect.

"See you tomorrow," he said, and I watched his back vanish into the night.

I slipped into the house, hoping Mom wouldn't be around. Music trickled down from her room. I needed to tell her I was sorry for storming out on her. Sorry we didn't get along better. I almost opened her door when I heard Jack's voice and changed my mind. It would have to wait.

14
Balancing

I fixed breakfast for Mom and Jack, and they left for work. No remarks about our conversation last night or anything more about my working another day. And I wasn't about to ask, because I wanted the day free to be with Peter.

As the Volvo drove off and I wiped my hands on the dishrag, I knew I'd need to talk with her. *Tonight*, I promised myself and God. I'd try to clear things up.

Peter and I met at the pasture and went to the beach, me on Khan, him on his skateboard. "Feeling better?" he asked.

I nodded. "I still have to talk to her more, but I'm not so upset. You looked really tired last night," I added. "Are you okay?"

His skateboard rumbled beside me, and he put his hand on my knee, slowing him down to a roll alongside us. "Sometimes the classes get exhausting. But it's okay. It makes you a better dancer."

"Have you ever hurt yourself?"

"Oh, sure. Pulled muscles and the like. But I've been lucky"—*Do Christians have luck?* I wondered—"because my instructors have been careful. Some teachers push the kids, especially little girls, to dance on *pointe* before they are able. But Matthew, my teacher, is concerned with balancing one's life. He wants us to be dancers, not only performers."

I liked that. Despite what Mom said, Dad wanted balance in our lives, too. Sure the horses were really first for Dad and me, but other things were important. The family. Friends. Of course, God. I smiled ruefully. If I were honest, I knew God often was second place to the horses. Balancing one's life wasn't easy.

The Sparkle rolled on the early morning waves, nosing against the slip.

"You get in," said Peter, "and lead Khan up beside the slip. See that island?" He pointed. It rose from the sea like a rocky palm of a giant's hand. "We can swim Khan out there. Sometimes you can see sea lions and dolphins," he said.

"I guess if she should flounder, we can still pull her along," I said.

"Sure. *The Sparkle* is powerful. Besides, the island isn't more than a quarter of a mile away. Khan can swim that."

I got into the boat, tugging the lead line until Khan moved up, chest deep, beside the boat. She stared curiously at us. Peter untied the ropes mooring us and started the engine.

Khan flared her nostrils and pricked her ears. Peter guided *The Sparkle* out.

"Come on, Khan," I said. Move."

She resisted, her head and neck stretching out like a bow, the lead line an arrow. "Khan!" I wrapped the end of the rope around a metal mooring knob sunk in the boat's side and let the boat itself drag the mare.

She suddenly came, plunging into the icy water, snorting. A smile filled my face. First a whale, now a horse attached to the boat.

127

"How's she doing?" called Peter as he guided the boat toward the island.

"Okay." Her mane and tail waxed silver on the greenish surface, and her breathing puffed up. It was odd to hear her out on the sea. Khan swam easily to the island, unalarmed, as if we did this every day. Craggy rocks rose up from the breaking waves of white. Clumps of grass clung to the stones, and a few gulls lifted off, squawking angrily at us.

"I'm going to pull the boat up onto that sandy spit, so you can jump on out and lead Khan. It's shallow," he said.

Khan struck the sand first and drew herself up, the water shivering off her. Then the boat hit the sand, and Peter killed the engine. Waves slapped me as I jumped out and landed hip deep. Khan pulled me out of the water and onto the shore. "Good girl," I told her and patted her, especially her legs, to be sure she hadn't cut them on any hidden rocks.

Peter tied *The Sparkle* to an outcropping of mossy stones and pulled out a backpack and canteen. "There's a little beach around the rocks," he said and started out on a narrow dirt trail, the canteen bouncing at each stride. I followed with Khan ambling after me.

The beach *was* little. Only a few feet across and sand ran up to the sheer cliff that towered above us, the highest point of the island. A few pelicans flapped up and headed to the pier.

"Why don't you let her go? She can't get away unless she swims," he said, "There's grass on top of the rocks."

So I pulled off the hackamore, and Khan slowly wheeled around, sniffing at the sand so grains flew up. Then she went down, rolling and grunting. We had to jump out of the way as she thrashed and finally scrambled up. She shook herself like a dog, sand spattering, then she bolted over the path and vanished around the edge of the cliff.

"I guess she didn't like our company," I said. Peter sat on the sand and slipped off his backpack and canteen.

"It's okay," he said. "I like your company, if that's any consolation."

My face grew warm, but I teased back. "Maybe a little."

He drank from the canteen and handed it to me. Farley would have shrieked, *Cooties! Germs!* But I took the flat metal canteen, covered with thin green material, and was conscious that his lips had just been on the mouth of the canteen. I drank, wishing instead we were kissing.

I wiped my mouth and handed him the canteen and knelt beside him in the sand.

It was hot under my bare knees. I let a handful sift between my fingers, smooth and dry.

"Sometimes Laing and I dive here," he said. "Once we saw a hammerhead shark. It must have been as long as a car. I was pretty scared."

"That guy that Abalone scared off thought she was a shark," I said.

"I wonder where she is," said Peter.

I wonder, too. But I said the right thing, "I hope she's with her pod, safe and happy."

"Don't you wish she'd stay around? And be like a pet?"

"All the time." We looked at each other and smiled. "I've even prayed that she'd come back, but I know that's pretty selfish."

"Yeah, probably. Maybe there will be whales in heaven."

Horses, too, please, Lord. "I hope so."

"Call her," he suddenly urged. "Whales and dolphins have terrific hearing."

"How should I call for her?"

"How did you call when the guy was bothering you?"

"But I didn't," I said. "It just happened."

"Maybe. Just say her name."

So I called, "Abalone! Abalone!" and the wind snatched my words, hurtling them over the water. I had a quick image of her coming to me and me throwing my arms around her black, rubbery head. What power, if animals truly came when I called! But she didn't swim up.

So instead we walked around the island, which was only about the size of an elementary schoolyard. The island bulged at the far end, as if someone had squeezed the other side. Khan grazed on the slope, flicking her tail at the gnats.

Peter and I waded in the tide pools. Lots of urchins hung onto the rocks, and when I put my finger in them, they tightened down and squirted water at me. A bit of iridescence caught my attention, so I reached for it and brought it up, dripping. Outside it was knobby and green, but when I turned it over the sunlight shimmered across it. Half of an abalone shell. I rubbed it with my finger and thought it was like life. Inside, like the mother-of-pearl, the shell was sparkly like Jesus promised, but outside it was ugly like the world.

I put it into my pocket. I was getting closer to finding a whole abalone shell.

Peter splashed into the water, his clothes on the shore. "Come on in," he said. "It's not too cold."

Slowly I pulled off my clothes, self-conscious, wanting to hide behind rocks even though I had my bathing suit on under my shorts and shirt.

Even with my tennis shoes on, the rocks were slippery, and carefully I waded out until I was swimming. Khan came down to the tide pools and whinnied, shaking her head. I hoped she wouldn't come in.

Peter laughed.

"What's so funny?" I asked, starting to swim back in so I could grab her if she decided she'd swim. She whickered and stood so the waves lapped up her black hoofs.

Peter still had a big grin on his face and was pointing behind me. I turned and saw her. Abalone.

15
Island Dance

She came. *You came.* Like magic.

She creaked, her open mouth showing smooth, round teeth. Her head bumped my arm like firm marble. "What have you been up to?" I asked her, and she just said another string of creaks, like old hinges and a shortwave radio. "Why aren't you safe with your pod?"

A latticework of white lines ran over her back, under her belly and around her dorsal fin, but they didn't look infected or puffy. She slapped her fin, and wash sprayed up over me.

"Hey!" I splashed her back, and she rolled and dived. When she came up, she was farther out and squealing again.

"Follow you? Is that it?" I swam to her side, and she dipped her dorsal fin against me. I took hold, catching my breath, and she shot away, cutting through the water effortlessly. After a few moments I let go, and she circled back to me.

"Where are you taking me?" I asked her as she tipped her fin and poked me in the chest with it. "My mother told me to never take rides with strangers."

An incredible joy assaulted me. "But you're not a stranger. Not anymore!" I took hold of her fin, and she vaulted through the water, faster than Peter's boat.

The island grew small, and I let go again, afraid. Abalone faced me, her mouth tipped in the perpetual smile. "What about Peter? He'll worry, don't you think?"

She creaked, as though answering me very precisely. Waves rolled us up and down, and when I got tired of treading water I reached out and clung to her side. She didn't take me for another ride; instead we remained quiet together, listening to the ocean mutter.

In the peaceful stillness I could almost imagine I was a pilot whale. Perhaps not only will there be whales in heaven, but maybe we'll be able to shape change. Be a whale. Then a swift shiver and become a horse. Another shudder and transform into a star.

A star. My dreams rose around me. The brown dwarves. The wicked face. Abalone was a cool comfort. *Chase away my nightmares.* I wanted her to be thoroughly magic and powerful. *Save me!* But I knew it couldn't be so. Only One can really save.

I stroked her sides, holding on with one hand to keep from having to tread water. Her skin rolled off under my fingers as I rubbed.

"I have to tell Mom about you," I said. "And what you mean, and how I think God is with us both. Even if Mom sends me home, forbids me to ever go to the beach again, I just have to tell her."

I knew she wouldn't understand, and I wanted to weep, but there was more seawater around me than I had in me.

My body trembled. "We should go back," I said. "Peter will be worrying."

She still didn't move, so I began to swim away from her to the island. She followed, creaking, scolding, and slapped me gently with her fin. The last time I'd been spanked was fifth grade! She offered me her fin and when I gripped it, she sailed back to the island, not moving as fast as before. Twice her body sort of jerked, like a twitch of muscles, and I almost let go, afraid I was somehow hurting her, but then she'd recover and keep swimming.

"Emily!" called Peter. He swam out to meet us. "She took you so far."

Abalone held still and let Peter pet her and lean against her, but she didn't offer him her fin. And I had the feeling it wasn't because she didn't want to or didn't like him. She acted tired, like the colts do after being weaned from their dams. A little dazed.

I got out of the water and lay down in the warm sand, my towel over me, and watched Peter laze around with Abalone. She creaked at him and rubbed up beside him. Khan had returned to grazing, her ears flickering in our direction.

"Pinch me," called Peter. "I think I'm dreaming."

"Don't worry. It's real," I said. "The real reality."

Abalone dived, her flukes flipping into the air, and vanished. Far out, farther than she'd taken me, I thought I saw her surface, but then the dark line was gone. Peter came in and lay down next to me.

"It's a mini-miracle," he said.

"Maybe it's a whole miracle."

He smiled and threw his arm over me. "Do you have a boyfriend?" he asked.

What a question! "No, not really." There was a guy back home I had been sort of interested in, but after the first fluttery moments we'd settled down to being buddies. "Do you have a girl friend?" I asked.

"Nothing serious." Translated, that meant there was a girl he liked, but perhaps she didn't like him as much.

I've had lots of crushes, but they never amounted to much except sweaty palms and pounding hearts. I wished Peter would kiss me again. I wished I were braver, and I'd kiss him. Instead he removed his arm and sat up. "You're really into Khan, aren't you?" he asked.

Talk about thought shifts. "Yeah, I'm really into horses. I guess it's a lot of who I am."

"Does anyone ever tell you that you're wasting your time?"

"Oh, yeah. Like my mom. Like people in my Sunday school class at home."

He began to smile.

"Like a lot of people."

"Do you think you're wasting your time?"

"What is this? Exam time?"

He shook his head. "I thought you might feel like I do. About my dance. I catch a lot of flak from people, too. Like they say, 'Why don't you go work in Mexico on spring break and help the poor people there instead of dancing in *Swan Lake* or doing those horrible rock videos?'"

"That's pretty rude," I said.

"I know. I feel like telling them to bark at the moon. It's not their business, really."

I rested my head on my outstretched arms. The sand scratched my belly as I resettled. "My dad says that riding the horses is God given, just like anything else, including plumbing or being a lawyer. Not everyone can train horses. And not everyone can dance."

"My dad thinks I'm a sissy," he said suddenly. "He never comes out and says that, but I know that's what he thinks."

"You're not a sissy." After all he'd done with Abalone!

Peter smiled, his eyes the color of the sea at dawn.

"I want to see you dance," I said. "Right now."

"Really?"

"Yes."

"Without music, it's a little weird." He stood, thinking. "I'll do part of my solo for *The Firebird*. It's a dance written by my instructor. He's really good."

I sat up, smiling at him.

He bowed low to me. "I will do the lady's bidding," he said.

Slowly he moved, stretching his arms and legs as if he were awakening. The sunlight was his partner. He danced with fierce concentration. Precise. Clean. Like a well-trained dressage horse, he flowed with infinite grace.

He swooped low, next to me. "Join me."

"I can't dance!"

"Of course you can. What have you been doing with Khan and Abalone all this time?"

Playing. Loving them.

"Dancing is joy in motion." He pulled me to my feet. I never went to school dances or anything, although Melissa and I used to practice dancing in front of her full-length mirror. He began moving to the music in the wind and the sea, and I followed him.

He came closer to me, and I put my arms around his neck. I thought my heart would leap from me as he kissed me. I didn't want the dance to end.

We swam Khan back without any problem. I kept looking back for Abalone. Peter teased me, "Can't keep your eyes off me, huh?"

"Hardly," I said and flicked some water at him. He flicked water back.

By the time I finished with Khan, Peter had left for SLO and a dance rehearsal, and the sun was low. The Volvo was in the driveway, and Biscuit and Jack were out on the lawn, Jack barefoot and Biscuit wandering without a leash.

"Hello, Emily," he said. "You look sunburned."

I held out my arms. They were turning red. "I hardly ever burn," I said. "I was out all day, though."

"Beth's fixing pasta."

"I'll go in and help her," I said.

But when I got inside, Mom wasn't fixing dinner. She was sitting at the kitchen table looking through a box of photos. "Look at this," she said and held up a picture. Instantly it swept me back to Christmas when I was eleven. Dad had hitched up two horses to a homemade wagon, and Ian and I had tied bells on the harness. It had been our last Christmas together.

"Yeah," I said. I sat down next to her and held the picture in my palm. "I remember the colts' names—Gem Boy and Klinger."

Mom shook her head, but she smiled. "You would remember that."

We dug through the photos.

"Here's Farley. He's only a baby."

"Here's your rocking horse. Remember how you cried because you wanted a real horse?"

Jack came in the door. "Where's dinner?" he mock-roared.

"Get it yourself! Emily and I are having too much fun."

And we were. Piles of memories were stacked beside us, and we talked about the past and it made it seem more real. Like there had been a time when we were a normal family and everyone pretty much loved each other.

Jack finished the pasta salad, served us, and went to eat in the living room. He snapped the VCR on and stuck in a war movie.

I drew a deep breath. "Mom?"

She looked up, questioning.

"I'm sorry about last night. You know, yelling at you, accusing you."

Her eyes softened, like they used to when Farley or I would fall down and skin our knees on the blacktop. "It's been the hardest on you, hasn't it?" she asked gently.

Tears pressed to my eyes, but I didn't want to start crying, because if I began I might not stop. I didn't want to do that. Not yet. I still had things to say.

"Well, it's been hard on all of us. Ian just buried himself in his schoolwork. And Farley, well, he used to cry and sometimes come and sleep with me, but he's okay now."

"And you?"

What about me? I was like an abalone shell, all closed up tight, nothing getting in or out, just my rough, ugly shell showing. "I guess I'm still pretty angry."

"I felt so guilty at first," said Mom. "Like I was the horrible one, since it was me who moved out. But I realized that John had left me years before."

"How do you mean?" I asked, almost not wanting to break the spell of her talking to me like an equal, like a peer, and not some dumb kid.

She shrugged and put the photos back into the box. "Keep this one?" she asked. The Christmas photo. I found I did want it.

"John and I found less and less to talk about. It sounds trite, but it's true. He was absorbed in the horses, and I needed something more."

"Have you found something more?"

She smiled slowly. "I'm not sure. Sometimes I have, sometimes I don't think so."

"I know you think Christianity is sort of weird," I began, and she interrupted.

"No, I don't. But I do think getting too involved is a mistake."

"Well, whatever. But what I mean is, even though things aren't perfect, I found what I'm looking for in Jesus."

"You sound like an old roommate of mine."

"Who?"

"Candy Evans. You met her once, remember? She was a real Jesus freak. But in a nice way."

I laughed. "Am I a Jesus freak in a nice way?"

"Yes, I think so."

I guess if your own mother was going to think you were a freak, it was good at least to be a nice freak! "I want to tell you that I saw the pilot whale again."

Alarm sprang into her face. "Emily, I told you—"

"Wait," I said. "It's fine, really. She's gentle, Mom. But I want to tell you that to me she has been a gift from God. Really. Maybe that sounds dumb, but I thought I should tell you that I was with her, because I know it scares you."

"If you know it scares me, why tell me?"

It was hard to explain. "I guess I just want to be honest."

"I appreciate that, Emily. But as your mother I'm going to tell you to leave that whale alone."

I knew she wouldn't change her mind, but somehow I could bend this time. "I know," I said. She looked surprised. "I'll leave her alone if that's what you want. But she really is safe."

"I find that hard to believe, gift from God or not."

I felt like a newly broke colt, bit heavy in my mouth and the strange weight of a person on my back. But for a colt it was necessary to be broken. And perhaps for people, too.

"Thanks for showing me the pictures," I said. "I'm going to go read for awhile."

"Still reading those endurance books?"

"Yeah, the race is only in ten days." That was a scary thought. I got up and headed for the stairs.

"Em?" Her voice circled me like a rope. I looked back, and she said. "I'm glad you told me about the pilot whale."

"I thought you should know." And I wondered if she would change from a brown dwarf to an average, but wonderful, G-type star like the sun. I hoped so. And if prayers meant anything. . . .

Upstairs I tried to read, but my thoughts drifted back to the sea, the warm sun, Peter's arms like a line of warmth across my back, and his kisses. Life would be easier if we were horses or pilot whales. We'd just run off together, and no one would think it wrong.

It wasn't easy being a human. I smiled, thinking about what my brothers would say to me if I came up with that remark.

But even though it wasn't easy, I was glad I was a person and not an animal.

At least most of the time.

16
The Black Swan

The next ten days galloped by. Any other time when I would be waiting for something, like a horse show, a party, or a phone call from a boy, the time crept. But race day suddenly appeared, fogless and bright, and Khan and I were entered whether we were ready or not.

Peter rode with me to the starting place, jogging on Seal. "You've done all that you can," he said. "Now it's up to Khan and her genetic makeup. That's all."

I couldn't help it. I laughed. He gave me a startled look. "What?"

"Is that what you think before you dance? That it's out of your control now and depends on your genes?"

"I guess not." He gave me a rueful smile. "That did sound dumb. What I meant was, you've done everything you can. You can't do any more than try your best. And I do think *that* before I audition or perform."

As we drew closer to the big pasture about three miles from See Canyon, Khan tossed her head. She vibrated. She was saying, *A race? Are we really going to race?* So maybe she did understand the words I'd whispered into her mane this morning, sort of half a prayer, half an explanation to her, *You'll be racing soon. And if you don't win it's okay. I still love you.*

But it would be nice to win and show them all what we can do. "Them all" was Mom, mostly. But since we'd talked the Night of the Photos, she'd been more relaxed and didn't even ask me to work an extra day at Sea Breeze. A relief. And I'd kept my end of the bargain and hadn't looked for Abalone. I'd only gone to the beach a couple times with Peter to swim Khan. The rest of the time we'd spent in the hills. But my heart had been out to sea, hoping the pilot whale truly had gone home.

"Look at the horses," said Peter, breaking me out of my thoughts.

Heavy oak trees surrounded the fence line, but beyond the trees horses and riders milled. Hundreds of horses. Khan whinnied shrilly.

A man at the gate held up his clipboard. "Name?" he asked us. I told him, and he checked off my name and handed me two squares of plastic with the number 743 printed in red. I pinned one square to the front of my shirt, and Peter leaned between our horses and pinned the other on my back.

"How many people are registered?" Peter asked.

"About two hundred." The man put his hand on Khan's hip, spoke kindly to her, and with a narrow paintbrush wrote my number in red on both of her hips. She stood still and only swished her tail hard once.

"Pretty mare," he said and tossed the brush into a bucket of water. "She's a different-looking Arabian."

"Polish Arabian," I said.

"A lot of the horses entered are Arabian or half Arabian," he said and patted Khan again. "The race will start in forty-five minutes. Go on in and feel free to warm her up. If you have any questions, look for someone wearing a Black Swan T-shirt."

Yeah, I had questions. Like will I win? Will I make a complete fool of myself? Peter and I rode through the gate. Behind us were others, and the man was checking them in, too.

Riders loped horses in circles. People were saddling. Grooming. Shouting. Horses snorted. Whinnied. Bucked. Khan tossed her head again, excited.

I patted her, hoping to contain my own nervousness, holding it at bay in my brain, and not letting the fear leak into my body where Khan would sense it and get frantic.

It wasn't easy.

"Let's go under that tree there," said Peter and steered us to an oak tree, probably as old as the earth. The shade was soothing after the fiery sun. I slid off Khan to rest her. Peter tied Seal to a branch. Khan wanted to graze, too, but I didn't want her to have any more food in her belly than her early breakfast. She'd drop her head and I'd haul her face back up until she laid her ears back at me.

"Sorry," I said. "It's just the way it is."

The time crept by now. It was the longest forty-five minutes I'd ever spent. Finally a man with a bullhorn rode into the pasture on a bright bay gelding. "All riders line up. Line up, riders."

"I guess that means me."

"I guess it does."

I checked the hackamore and straightened the reins.

"Well, I can't tell you what the dancers tell each other," he said.

"Why?"

"They say, 'Break a leg.' That sounds pretty bad."

"I'll say it does."

"But good luck. I'll ride Seal over to the finish line."

"Mom and Jack'll be there, too."

"I'll look for them."

He wrapped his arms around me. "I'll give you a proper victory kiss later."

"And if I don't win?" I was pretty sure we wouldn't now. Too many horses.

"I'll consider alternatives." He smiled.

I slugged him and vaulted onto Khan's back.

I didn't look back, but rode to the fluttering orange ribbons at the starting line. The instructions had read that the nine-mile path would be marked with more orange ribbons. No one was allowed a chance to examine the course first, and no checkpoints were held. You just raced straight through. Vets were around—I'd seen Dr. Myers, who'd examined Khan.

So many horses.

"Big crowd, isn't it?" A woman on a Paint with strange, blue eyes walked up to us.

I nodded, frantically.

"Don't worry. Most of them drop back in a hurry."

I hoped I wouldn't be one of them.

Some riders around us, like the man in front on a large, rawboned chestnut, were serious looking. Expensive tack. Horses with braided manes and tails. Should I have done that to Khan? Too late now.

Most people, though, laughed and talked and looked as if they were having fun. My heart rate slowed down.

The center of the field vanished and only horses sprouted up. I sneezed from the dust.

"Line up!" shouted the man with the bullhorn. The wind couldn't touch me, because so many bodies surrounded us. *So this is what a wild horse herd must feel like.*

"When the gun fires, the race begins," said the starter. His words wriggled in the air. "May the best horse and rider win."

144

A pause, quiet. The horses seemed to sense the moment and everyone froze, suspended. The gun exploded.

Khan went straight up. Instinctively I must have known what she'd do, for I clung tight and she didn't unseat me. Stupid me for not practicing starts, knowing her past. Then she sprang forward, and I realized she wasn't rearing, but breaking fast. Super fast.

The trail jumped up onto the first hill, and I drove Khan straight up, threading around other riders. True to the lady on the Paint's words, some of the pack dropped back.

People held back their horses to merge onto the narrow path, like it was a freeway or something. We wouldn't win by waiting, so I guided Khan off the path and we trotted past the mob through the grass.

A few others rode off the path, too. Khan swung up the hill in good time, despite the rough ground. I watched for gopher holes and rocks. At the top of the hill, the path crossed between trees, and I drew her back to the marked path and followed orange ribbons, leading us higher and higher. Briefly the ocean glinted, then vanished as we dropped through a narrow valley of rocks.

Lots of riders had dropped back after the first hill. Hadn't they even practiced? But not everyone is as obsessive as me. Until today, I hadn't been aware how badly I wanted to win. The thought of losing choked me, yet I had to face that it might happen. Lots of horses were in front of us.

According to my watch, only four minutes and ten seconds had gone by. A lifetime.

The hills grew steeper. Of course, the middle of the race. Halfway through. Sweat flecked Khan's shoulders and flanks. Not bad. We passed a dark bay mare, her body lathered.

145

Orange ribbons beckoned us up the stern, granite covered ridge. Khan slowed to a jog, and I let her pick her way, her head low, ears alert. She passed two more horses.

Off the ridge, Khan slid down the embankment. A horse in front went to his knees, and we dodged them as the rider yanked the horse's head up.

Eleven minutes and fifty-three seconds.

The course doubled back on itself, heading for the sea and the finish line on the beach. We charged through a valley and overtook a man on a liver bay. The man grimaced as we galloped past him. How many people were in front of us? Twenty? More? Trees obscured my vision.

Khan breathed harder, but she pushed her nose against the hackamore and I let her out a bit. She stretched and caught two more riders, women in fancy English saddles. I felt like the poor scullery maid, bareback on a wild-looking mare, but I was in front. I smirked. Unkind, I know. But the race wasn't over yet, I sternly told myself. Smirk later if there's cause.

Orange ribbons whizzed by. We thundered for the sea. The heavy earth-churned scent faded, and a briny smell filled the air. Khan increased her stride, her mane in my face.

We crossed the highway. The race crew had road-blocked it in both directions and laid about a foot of sand over the asphalt. Khan hesitated midpoint, then leaped. Her hooves struck the hard surface. Great. Just what she needs, to hit the blacktop at thirty miles an hour. But she kept running without a hitch.

A pack of riders struggled through deep sand. Khan swept by them. All the hours of trotting in sand paid off.

Fifteen minutes and forty-two seconds.

Sweat oozing down her back made me slide. I

tightened my legs. They ached, but not badly. We galloped around the bluff where Laing's house squatted. I could almost hear his laughter, but it was only the roar of the sea. Another rider fell behind us. At the firmer wetter sand, Khan shifted into a faster gallop. The desert mare at the sea. She drank the wind. She flew. She was the most wonderful creature in the world.

Seventeen minutes.

Only three riders galloped in front of us. A bay, a chestnut, and a liver-spotted Appy. We had to catch them. *We can win. We can really win!*

The finish line fluttered with orange ribbons. Bleachers rose up like cupped hands on either side of the line, and the crowd cheered, sounding like frantic gulls.

And then I saw her. Abalone. Floating in the sea only five feet from us.

17
Abalone Again

I began to haul back on the reins, race or no race, but Peter shouted, his voice strong as thick glass, "Don't, Emily! Win the race!"

He was right. Stopping now wouldn't help Abalone. I flung myself against Khan's neck, and she bolted after the leaders. Tears blinded me for a moment. Tears from the wind. The cutting sea wind.

Eighteen minutes and fifteen seconds.

My thoughts streamlined into concentrating on the race. I pretended I was Khan and tried to become part of her fiber, her hot racing body.

Khan's nose was at the Appy's black tail. Then at his flanks. His ribs. His shoulders. On past him, with a surge like a kite broken from its string, Khan fled.

The bay and the chestnut raced side by side. Nineteen minutes and five seconds.

"Go, Khan, go," I cried and she strained, galloping mightily. She caught up to the two, her flared red nostrils at their rumps. The finish line closed in. My heart pounded so loud I couldn't hear anything else.

Khan plummeted over the sand, pulling past the two horses, and poked her nose in front, then her head. We hit the finish line one length in the lead.

Flashbulbs popped in front of us as I slowed Khan. She half reared as a photographer ran under her nose, taking our picture.

"Hey, aren't you the kid that cut the whale free? What do you think? Is that her dead over there?"

I turned Khan away to the shore and trotted her back, out of the way of the other racers, the water frothing up between her legs.

Dead? Could she really be dead? Not many seemed to notice the body bobbing in the surf. A Coast Guard cutter was coming around the bluff. How long had she been here?

I drove Khan out into the breakers and halted her chest deep. The whale had crisscrosses of white scars over her dorsal fin. *Why?* Why was she dead?

Mike, the reporter who had interviewed Peter and me, waded out. "I heard the report on the radio," he said. "Is it the same pilot whale?"

"Yeah," I said.

"I'm really sorry," he said, but he kept taking my photo.

Suddenly I wanted to get away. I didn't dare make Khan gallop; she was still breathing hard. I rode her out of the water. The Coast Guard boat came closer. I knew what they'd do next. Shoot a harpoon into her and tow her back where an autopsy would be done. *Tow her.*

More riders galloped along the sand toward the finish line. I slipped off Khan and walked her back. As I grew closer to the bleachers, Mom walked to me.

She didn't say one word to me, only opened her arms, and I went to her, dry-eyed, thinking very clearly that brown dwarves were stars that had nothing to give, not even to themselves. But she gave to me, in the tightness of her arms, and I knew that she was a star in change.

That night Peter and I sat in the basement, me on my belly, conked out, but not willing to go to sleep. Too wired. Dawn sat beside Peter, who stretched out. She tried to stretch her fat legs, but only succeeded in falling over with a furious grunt.

"I just wish there was someone to get mad at. Someone to punch out," I said. "Instead there's nothing. Just Abalone dead."

"Maybe they'll know more after they examine her."

That was gross. I loved that whale, and I didn't want them hurting her body, even though she was beyond hurt now. I just hoped she was in heaven.

"I would have blown the race if you hadn't yelled at me to go on," I said.

Peter lifted his head. "What are you talking about?"

A chill went through me. "You know," I started to say, but then I realized there was no way I could have heard Peter. No one was around. The bleachers had been a good twenty lengths away when I heard his voice.

"No, I don't know," he said quietly and picked up Dawn. She tried to stretch again and fell over.

I told him what had happened without any exaggeration. "Maybe I imagined it," I said.

"Maybe not," he said just as quietly. "Sometimes strange things happen when people care for each other."

"My older brother likes to say that all things are connected to each other," I said.

"I don't doubt it." Dawn had crawled over his legs and lay there making noises and drooling.

"If it's okay with my dad, I want to give some of the prize money to one of those groups who help whales and dolphins," I said.

"Five hundred dollars is a lot of money," he said. "You're rich and famous."

"Hardly." Famous, maybe. That Mike guy had kept calling me on the phone until Mom unplugged the lines.

I rolled over and sat up, yawning, brushing my hair out of my eyes. "I'm not sure if I should celebrate or be depressed," I said. "Why can't things be simple?"

"Some things are," he said and kissed me. Dawn looked up at me, her funny eyes sparkling.

"Hos," she said. Then, "Em."

"That's my name! Good girl."

"We've been practicing," he said and took me into his arms. Dawn wriggled out from between us and stared at herself in the mirror, laughing.

Abalone filled my thoughts, even as Peter held me. Maybe I would see her again someday. Until then, I'd look for her in the shards of abalone I found on the beach. Perhaps I would still find a complete, intact shell, one with the most shimmery insides. The iridescence of abalone.

Leave Beedee . . . Never!

Good-bye, Beedee

Marcia Stallings is a horse lover. But Dad says they have to leave the ranch and move to Kansas City—into a cramped, ugly apartment. And worse, he's marrying a woman who doesn't know anything about horses! Dad says it's all for the best, but how can it be?

Once Over Lightly

Marcia's life is just about perfect. A job at Gatlin Stables and a chance to compete in horse shows are dreams come true. Then Marcia meets handsome Barry Warwick, and life isn't so perfect anymore. Why does he take an instant dislike to her? Could he be the one sabotaging her work?

Oklahoma Summer

A whole summer back on her grandparents' ranch! But things have changed. The work is hard, the weather's hot, and Marcia doesn't trust Lester, the ranch hand, who seems to hate horses. Even her old friends have changed. Then Barry Warwick arrives and Marcia's summer has a different look. . . .

NORMA JEAN LUTZ, author of the Marcia Stallings books, is a free-lance writer. She lives in Tulsa, Oklahoma.

Chariot Books
David C. Cook Publishing Co.

New dreams to dreams . . .

Reach with all Your Heart
Angie and Con have dreams—first college and then a new life together far from their Los Angeles neighborhood of peeling paint, dirt, and exhaust fumes. Con's way out will be a college scholarship. And Angie's, too, he said. They'd do it together—just like they always had.

Then a terrible accident almost costs Con his life, and Angie's world is shattered. Can God use this tragedy to change their lives and give them new dreams?

For more about life one Angie's and Con's street, read:

A Place to Belong
Somebody Special to Love

MARILYN CRAM DONAHUE, author of these books, has lived in Southern California all her life and writes about the Los Angeles neighborhoods and people she knows so well.

Chariot Books
David C. Cook Publishing Co.

Working together as a team . . . would it ever happen?

Andrea's Best Shot

Andrea's last year at Brown Junior High might be good after all. With a new coach, who also teaches Andrea's Sunday school class, the girls' basketball team is off to a great start. So is Andrea's relationship with Matt.

But Andrea is worried about the way her friend Jill has been acting since she started to hang around the new girl from the air force base. It could ruin their friendship—and wreck the whole team's chance to enter their first tournament ever.

Dawn's Diamond Defense

Dawn discovers that learning good defense in soccer reaps more benefits than just winning a game. But two black eyes and a date with a good-looking sophomore is a strange way to start the season.

DAN JORGENSEN, author of these two books, is active in sports and journalism. He lives in Minnesota with his wife and two daughters.

Chariot Books
David C. Cook Publishing Co.

This book
belongs to
Ruth V.-N.